A shotgun b
banister

The Executioner ducked out of sight as more bullets peppered the walls and ceiling overhead.

Barging through the first door on his right, he found himself inside what looked like a guest room. Directly opposite the doorway where he stood, a sliding door opened onto a narrow balcony that faced the yard and street beyond. It was a drop of twenty feet, and then a run of twenty yards across the lawn. He would be wide open to the shooters in the house—and any who were quick enough to follow him.

One step at a time.

Bolan kicked the bedroom door shut, locked it and crossed to the window. He opened it and waited for the angry voices to resume from the hallway. If they went straight, he had a chance to make the drop unnoticed. But if they searched room by room…

The doorknob jiggled, and Bolan stitched a double 3-round burst across the paneling, and was rewarded with a squeal of pain. A second later, he was on the balcony, one leg across the rail.

As small-arms fire ripped through the room's door and eastern wall, Bolan took his leap of faith.

MACK BOLAN ®
The Executioner

The Executioner®
Don Pendleton's
BATTLE CRY

A GOLD EAGLE BOOK FROM
WORLDWIDE®

TORONTO • NEW YORK • LONDON
AMSTERDAM • PARIS • SYDNEY • HAMBURG
STOCKHOLM • ATHENS • TOKYO • MILAN
MADRID • WARSAW • BUDAPEST • AUCKLAND

For Tim Dinsdale (1924–1987)
and
Robert Henry Rines (1922–2009)

First edition January 2012

ISBN-13: 978-0-373-64398-1

Special thanks and acknowledgment to
Michael Newton for his contribution to this work.

BATTLE CRY

In the mind and nature of a man a secret is an ugly thing, like a hidden physical defect.

—Isak Dinesen
1885–1962
Last Tales

Some secrets are best left buried, with the men who keep them.

—Mack Bolan

THE
MACK BOLAN
LEGEND

Nothing less than a war could have fashioned the destiny of the man called Mack Bolan. Bolan earned the Executioner title in the jungle hell of Vietnam.

But this soldier also wore another name—Sergeant Mercy. He was so tagged because of the compassion he showed to wounded comrades-in-arms and Vietnamese civilians.

Mack Bolan's second tour of duty ended prematurely when he was given emergency leave to return home and bury his family, victims of the Mob. Then he declared a one-man war against the Mafia.

He confronted the Families head-on from coast to coast, and soon a hope of victory began to appear. But Bolan had broken society's every rule. That same society started gunning for this elusive warrior—to no avail.

So Bolan was offered amnesty to work within the system against terrorism. This time, as an employee of Uncle Sam, Bolan became Colonel John Phoenix. With a command center at Stony Man Farm in Virginia, he and his new allies—Able Team and Phoenix Force—waged relentless war on a new adversary: the KGB.

But when his one true love, April Rose, died at the hands of the Soviet terror machine, Bolan severed all ties with Establishment authority.

Now, after a lengthy lone-wolf struggle and much soul-searching, the Executioner has agreed to enter an "arm's-length" alliance with his government once more, reserving the right to pursue personal missions in his Everlasting War.

Prologue

Glasgow, Scotland: 9:18 a.m.

Galen Lockhart checked his Rolex Oyster Perpetual Milgauss watch and discovered that, against all odds, he was ahead of schedule. His hangover was fading slowly, and he knew it was a mere illusion that he still heard echoes of the music that had hammered him the previous night for hours, at the Barrowlands. After his steaming shower, there was no way he could still smell What's-her-name's perfume.

What *was* her name? Something vaguely exotic, he recalled. Finela or Grizela? Maybe Annabella?

Screw it.

She'd been gone when Lockhart had received his jarring wake-up call from the Hilton Glasgow's concierge. His wallet was still intact, and that was all that mattered. If he hurt a little here and there, it only meant they'd had a damn good time.

"A bonny day, this is," his guide declared.

Lockhart had never seen Craig Stewart when he wasn't smiling. Could it be some kind of surgical enhancement? Maybe he'd had a nip-tuck in the cheek muscles to lift the corners of his mouth in perpetuity?

Or was he just another jolly Scot?

Whatever, he was right about the day. Bright sunshine and a clear blue sky over the city, as their limo rolled along Cathedral Street toward Stirling Road. From there, it would be out of

Glasgow proper, into Springburn, where the ground breaking was scheduled to begin at ten o'clock.

The factory would mark SenDane's first move outside the States. Lockhart had bucked the tide of outsourcing as long as possible, but now the time had come to ride the wave, before he wound up drowning in red ink. And if the move got him some good publicity, well, what was wrong with that?

"Your parents must be proud," Stewart said through his smile.

His ancestors had gambled on a one-way ticket to America during the twenties, started out in New York City but wound up in Philadelphia and prospered there. Each generation built on what the last had done, took full advantage of technology as it evolved and learned to play the games that made success, if not a lead-pipe cinch, at least a reasonable expectation.

"They'll be here for the grand opening," Lockhart replied. "Next June, if we don't run afoul of any snags."

"You'll be snag-free," Stewart assured him. "Everything's been taken care of, top to bottom."

Meaning politicians, unions and whatever else might slow construction if the wheels weren't greased with cash. Once they were up and running, Lockhart would recoup his bribes in spades, but at the moment, every penny counted.

"The Lord Provost is coming?" Lockhart asked.

"Aye," Steward said. "He wouldn't miss it for the world. And we've got five out of the seven MPs coming in."

"Sounds good."

"A bonny day," Steward repeated. "Everybody happy as a pig in shite."

"WE'RE IN THE SHITE if anything goes wrong," Patrick Whishart said, huddled in the backseat of a blue Ford Focus stolen from the long-term parking lot at Glasgow International Airport, its license plates switched with a junker from a Paisley wrecking yard.

"So, don't let anything go wrong, then," Bobby Tennant answered from the shotgun seat, not bothering to turn and face Whishart. "We do the job and get the hell away. All right?"

"He's got no cover, then?" Hugh Ferguson inquired from the backseat.

"To watch him dig a hole?" Tennant was scornful. "Just the copper you see sittin' over there."

One uniform sat inside his panda car, watching reporters square away their cameras and microphones. The VIPs hadn't arrived yet, but they would be turning up within the next few minutes if they meant to start the show on time.

And if they didn't, Tennant's team would wait.

Reaching between his knees into a paper shopping bag, Tennant withdrew a Sterling L2A3 submachine gun and a curved double-column magazine holding thirty-four rounds of 9 mm Parabellum hollowpoint rounds. Keeping a cold eye on the policeman in his car, Tennant snapped the magazine into the SMG's receiver and racked a round into the chamber.

Behind him, he heard his two other men priming their weapons, an Uzi for Ferguson and an Armalite AR-18 assault rifle for Whishart. Their driver, Duncan Nilsen, had an Ingram MAC-10 machine pistol in his lap, but he was staying with the Focus when they made their move, to have it ready when the hit went down.

"Remember," Tennant said, "go for the targets first and leave the copper be unless he makes a run at you. We know he'll use the radio. Don't sweat it. Hit the Yank and anyone who's fawning over him, then get back to the car. Hear me?"

They heard him, and they'd heard it all before, at least a dozen times during their planning sessions for the strike. It was a relatively simple job, but still important to the cause. Outsiders had to know they couldn't make a fortune on the backs of honest Scots, even if they had ancient roots in local soil.

"Here comes a limo," Nilsen warned them.

Tennant turned in his seat to eye the limousine, a black Rolls-Royce Ghost. The license plate on its front bumper showed the Scottish government's royal coat of arms. Dark tinted windows hid its passengers from view, but Tennant recognized the car and knew who was inside.

"Take him or leave him," he advised the others. "Tag the Yank for sure, then drop his lackeys if it doesn't slow you down."

"Another limo," Nilsen said. "And two more coming up behind it."

"Council members, maybe some MPs," Tennant suggested. "Careful with them, when it starts. We have some friends there, and it wouldn't do to mess them up."

"They take their chances, kissing Lockhart's arse," said Ferguson.

"Just follow orders," Tennant cautioned him. "Don't feck this up by thinkin' for yourself."

"ALL READY, from the looks of it," Craig Stewart said.

The politicians had arrived ahead of schedule, jockeying for face time with the television cameras, grabbing their sound bytes before all eyes and lenses focused on the American whose symbolic homecoming meant jobs and a boost for the city's flagging economy. Every politician who turned out for the ground breaking would be claiming credit for it, getting in another bid for votes.

"You brought the shovel, right?" Lockhart asked. "Christ, I never thought of it till now."

"It's in the trunk," Stewart assured him. "Sterling silver, bright and shiny new."

The spade was silver-plated, and had cost a pretty guinea, even so. Once jabbed into the dirt, it would be mounted on a placard and retired. A souvenir for someone, probably the Lord Provost, to join the case of eighteen-year-old single-malt Glenlivet whisky he'd received as Lockhart's token of appreciation for a quarter of an hour on the dais.

Moments later, they were out and moving toward the stage, with Stewart carrying the shovel. Lockhart had his short speech memorized, the usual spiel about returning to his roots and honoring his heritage. He thought to himself that if anyone was dumb enough to think of SenDane as a philanthropic charity, more power to them.

On the dais, shaking hands, Lockhart could feel his hangover trying to reassert itself, but he suppressed it, plastered on a smile to match Stewart's and stepped up to the microphone.

The turnout wasn't large and didn't have to be. The cameras were what counted, catching every second of the show.

"My friends and fellow Scots—"

A ripple in the small crowd caught his eye, distracting Lockhart as he saw three men advancing, rudely shoving past the others who'd arrived before them, pressing toward the stage. He didn't recognize the guns at first, until the nearest one was pointed at his face.

"Look out!" somebody shouted from below. Too late.

Lockhart began to turn, raising the spade as if it could protect him, hearing screams and curses from the crowd. Then, all he heard was thunder.

All he felt was pain.

Mack Bolan's flight from New York City landed more or less
on time. The jumbo jet had lifted off from JFK eleven minutes late yet somehow beat the captain's own best estimate
for crossing the Atlantic. They'd traveled more than thirty-two
hundred miles overnight, across five time zones, and Bolan
had done it in coach.

It was good to stretch his legs again, to work the kinks out
of his neck and lower back.

He took his time passing along the jetway, following the
signs to Immigration and Passport Control. Upon arrival at
their destination, Bolan's fellow travelers formed lines, according to their nationality. The fast lanes were for British
subjects, residents of nations in the European Economic Area,
and the Swiss. All others joined the lines requiring more detailed interrogation by authorities.

Bolan was ready with his landing card and passport, this
one in the name of Matt Cooper from Los Angeles. Mr.
Cooper was on holiday with nothing to declare.

The immigration officer who beckoned Bolan forward
was a woman, pale and red-haired, with just the barest hint
of freckles on her nose. He would've had to guess about her
figure, since she was wearing body armor underneath her uniform, and her gunbelt had numerous black, bulky pouches.

She checked his face against the passport's photo, inquired

as to the purpose of his visit even though it was already indicated on his landing card, and asked for an address where he'd be staying while in Scotland.

Serving up the truth for once, Bolan replied, "No address. I'll be traveling and stopping where the spirit moves me, hoping there's a room available."

She frowned, then said, "Good luck with that" and slammed a stamp into his passport.

"Next!"

Glasgow International Airport, located eight miles southwest of the city's center, served more than seven million travelers per year. Most international arrivals passed through the main terminal, where two al Qaeda wannabes crashed a flaming Jeep Cherokee into the main pedestrian entrance on June 30, 2007. The Jeep failed to explode, but one of the men set himself afire and subsequently died in agony. His sidekick was arrested near the scene and pulled a thirty-two-year sentence for attempted murder.

So, security was tighter in the terminal these days. En route to claim his check-through suitcase, Bolan passed by teams of uniformed police in jaunty caps, with H&K MP-5 submachine guns slung across their chests. None of them paid particular attention to him, and he felt no sense of apprehension as he followed more signs to the baggage carousels on a lower level.

It wasn't cops who posed the main threat to his life from this point on.

His black, generic suitcase took another thirteen minutes to appear, but no one checked his luggage tag as Bolan headed for the kiosk where a hired car should be waiting for him. There, another woman with red hair— younger and more cheerful than the officer who'd stamped his passport—welcomed Bolan, found his reservation and received his California driver's license with a Platinum Visa, both once again in the name of Matt Cooper.

Bolan replied to the obligatory questions, lying where he needed to and staying vague about the rest. He took the lady up on her insurance offer—Bolan's rentals sometimes took a beating on the road—and opted for the prepaid "discount" refill of his gas tank when, or if, he managed to return the car.

There was, he thought, no reason why the rental company should eat the cost if something happened to their car while in his possession. The Visa card was solid, false name notwithstanding, and his debts were always paid on time, in full.

The ride selected for him was a gray Toyota Camry with a five-speed manual transmission, front-wheel drive, with a two-liter inline-four engine. Bolan put his suitcase in the spacious trunk and remembered that the driver's seat was on the right, the stick shift on his left.

As he left the car rental parking lot, with traffic rushing toward him on his right, Bolan quickly got the feel of it, his muscle-memory kicking in from other trips abroad, and he was on his way.

So far, so good. But Bolan couldn't leap into his mission as he was.

For starters, he was naked—or, at least, he felt that way, without a single weapon close at hand. Airline security made packing weapons on commercial flights unfeasible, and Bolan couldn't very well comply with standing rules for shipping lethal hardware in the baggage hold. Most of the gear that he relied on was legally off-limits to civilians in the States and the United Kingdom, so he'd traveled light, unarmed except for hands, feet and vast experience in taking life, up close and personal.

But he needed guns, perhaps explosives—and some information, too.

Thankfully, Bolan knew exactly where to find them in the heart of Glasgow, day or night.

IAN WATT WAS a respected businessman. Although he was a product of Gorbals—Glasgow's toughest slum, located on the south bank of the River Clyde—he'd risen far above his humble roots, like others he could name.

Gorbals owed its name to the Lowland Scots word for lepers, locally housed at Saint Ninian's Hospital in the fourteenth century and granted begging rights on nearby streets. Alumni of the district included some of Glasgow's most notorious characters, good and bad.

He had grown up on the streets, in essence, with the likes of Tam McGraw and Frank McPhee, both gone to their rewards now with a host of others who had battled through the ice cream wars and other skirmishes for turf across the years. Watt chose a slightly different path, fencing hot items through a pawn shop that had prospered and expanded into two, then four, then seven citywide. Most of his merchandise was perfectly legitimate.

Most, but not all.

Old friends and new acquaintances still had selected items that required a broker, and they needed other items to defend themselves from competition or the police. Firearms regulation in the British Isles had gone from bad to worse after the Dunblane massacre of 1996, in which sixteen children were killed in kindergarten class by a shooter who then killed himself. But life went on, and hardmen needed shooters all the same.

In Glasgow, many of them bought their wares from Ian Watt.

He had to watch out for the undercover filth, of course, but honestly, how hard was that? A few bob handed over, here and there, bought Watt a warning when the dogs were prowling in his neighborhood, and risks were minimized by dealing mainly with a trusted clientele.

Mainly.

Needless to say, there were exceptions to the rule, but all of them came recommended from another customer who'd dealt with Watt in other situations, with no comebacks. Like the fellow from America he was expecting for a nooner on this very day, referred to Watt by someone who knew someone else, and so it went.

And who was Watt, a thriving businessman, to turn away a foreign visitor in need?

Watt didn't care what use was ultimately made of any items he procured and sold on to the street. None of the weapons could be traced to him, either by registration numbers or the fancy stuff you saw on TV crime dramas. Watt never touched a piece or cartridge with his bare hands, damn sure never left his DNA on any item from his arsenal, and wouldn't take a fall for anything unless the coppers somehow found his basement arsenal.

Which wasn't very bloody likely, he thought.

At half-past eleven on the stroke, Watt put the Closed sign on his door and sent his pretty helper, Flora, off to lunch. She always took her time about it, likely making out with her boyfriend from the pizzeria down the street, but what of it? He'd hired her as eye candy, primarily, and got his money's worth when punters were distracted by her cleavage while he talked them down on loans, or jacked them up on retail prices. Best of all, she never questioned being sent out on some pointless errand or released ahead of closing time, as long as she was paid up for the day.

A perfect front, he thought, in all respects.

He smiled, amused as always by his own wry wit.

Watt didn't know exactly what his new customer had in mind, as far as shooters were concerned, but his inventory was extensive. Something for everyone, down in the basement— and twenty years to think about it at HMP Barlinnie, if he was caught with that kind of hardware on hand.

Unless, of course, he struck a deal to shift the burden somewhere else.

A dicey proposition, that was, if you thought about his customers. All men of honor, in their own eyes, meaning that they punished traitors harshly but might sell out their mothers if there was any profit in it.

Most of Glasgow's current so-called gangsters couldn't hold a candle to the old breed. They were tough enough, all right, but you could never tell when one of them might crack under interrogation. Once they got to thinking about prison and the things they'd have to do or do without inside, a lot of them would spill and put their best mates on remand.

Watt was a different sort, and anyone who mattered knew it, going in. It was a point of honor, and he knew what could become of those who snitched, even when they were certain that they'd gotten away with it. Watt, himself, hoped to die at ninety-something in a trollop's arms, rather than screaming on a rack somewhere.

When he had seen the back of Flora, Watt threw down a double shot of Royal Brackla whisky and felt the heat spread through his vitals, relaxing him from the inside out. First-timers always put his nerves on edge a little, but the whisky mellowed him like nothing else.

All ready to do this, he thought, and watched the big hand creep around toward twelve.

The shop on Dalhousie Street, in Garnethill, was closed when Bolan parked a half-block south of it, but he had been fore-warned of that. A knock on the glass door produced a slim man in his fifties, salt-and-pepper hair combed straight back from a craggy face that had absorbed its share of blows, and then some. His suit was Savile Row, though Bolan didn't know enough about the London fashion scene to peg a tailor.

The proprietor beamed a smile at Bolan through plate glass, then unlocked and opened the door. "Mr. Cooper, you would be?" he inquired.

Bolan nodded and said, "Mr. Watt?"

"In the flesh, sir. Come in, won't you please?"

Bolan scanned the merchandise while Watt secured the door behind him, checking out the street. He stocked a bit of everything, it seemed, from jewelry and musical instruments to antique silverware and china. Clearly, there was money to be made from someone else's disappointment.

"Just in from America, you'd be," Watt said as he returned,

no longer asking questions. "And looking for some tools of quality."

"Assuming that the price is right," Bolan replied.

"I take it that you understand our situation here. We haven't got a constitutional amendment giving us the right to carry guns, and all. The scrutiny is fierce."

"And yet."

"And yet. Of course. Just so you realize that heat increases costs for merchants *and* their customers."

"The money's not a problem," Bolan said.

"In that case," Watt replied, "please follow me. The merchandise you're looking for is kept downstairs."

He trailed Watt through a minioffice to a storage space in back, then down a flight of stairs concealed behind a steel door labeled Private—No Admittance. Watt turned on a bank of overhead fluorescent lights as they started their descent, bleaching the basement arsenal's beige paint and striking glints from well-oiled pieces of his secret stock.

The climate-controlled room measured right around three hundred square feet, running twenty feet long east to west, and fifteen wide, north to south. Within that space, Watt had collected an impressive cache of automatic weapons, shotguns, pistols and accessories for every killing need.

There was a .460 Weatherby Magnum for would-be elephant poachers, and a .50-caliber Barrett M-82 semiautomatic antimaterial rifle for hunters who wanted to bag an armored personnel carrier.

Speaking of big guns, Watt also stocked a 40 mm Milkor MGL 6-shot 40 mm grenade launcher, a Czech SAG-30 semi-auto launcher for smaller 30 mm grenades, and a South African Vektor Y3 AGL that required a tripod or vehicle mount for its full-auto spray of 280 grenades per minute.

"Much call for that in Glasgow?" Bolan asked his guide.

"If someone asks," Watt said, "I aim to please."

The remainder of his inventory was more convention, including various assault rifles, submachine guns and sidearms manufactured in Europe. Price tags were nowhere to be seen.

Bolan's first choice was a 5.56 mm Steyr AUG, the modern classic manufactured in Austria and carried by soldiers of twenty-odd nations, and by agents of U.S. Immigration and Customs Enforcement. Its compact bullpup design, factory-standard Swarovski Optik 1.5x telescopic sight, and see-through plastic magazines all made for a convenient, reliable combat rifle.

For backup and variety, Bolan next chose a Spectre M-4 submachine gun, manufactured at the SITES factory in Turin, Italy. Feeding 9 mm Parabellum cartridges from a four-column casket magazine, the Spectre carried fifty rounds to the average SMG's thirty or thirty-five. Its double-action trigger mechanism allowed safe carriage while cocked, and its muzzle was threaded for a suppressor, which Bolan added to his shopping cart.

Last up, for guns, he chose another Italian: the same selective-fire Beretta 93-R pistol that he favored in the States. It was no longer in production, but the piece Watt had acquired was brand-new in appearance, and a quick look proved it fully functional. In essence, with its muzzle brake, folding foregrip, and 20-round magazines, the 93-R gave Bolan a second SMG to play with. He picked a fast-draw shoulder rig to carry it, with pouches for spare magazines, and started shopping for grenades.

His choice there was the standard British L109 fragmentation grenade, a variant of the original Swiss HG 85 that had replaced the older L2A2 in the early 1990s. Each grenade weighed one pound and had a timed fuse, with a Mat Black Safety Clip similar to those found on American M-67 frag grenades.

Bolan bought an even dozen, just in case, added a KA-BAR fighting knife on impulse and decided he was done.

With ammunition, extra magazines and gun bags to conceal his purchases, the total was a flat eight thousand pounds. Say thirteen grand, in round numbers.

"I have a counteroffer for you," Bolan said.

"Not quite the way it works, friend," Watt replied.

"You haven't heard it, yet."

"Go on, then. Make me laugh."

Before Watt reached his pocket pistol, Bolan had the KA-BAR's blade against his throat.

"A name and address for your life," he said.

IT DIDN'T QUITE work out that way. Watt thought about it for a minute, then gave up the information Bolan needed, but it went against the grain. He could've simply spent the afternoon in handcuffs, in his soundproofed arsenal, but something in the Gorbals sense of "honor" made him try his hand against the Executioner, and Bolan left the KA-BAR stuck between the man's ribs to dam the blood flow, while he took another to replace it from the dealer's stash.

He left the shop with two gym bags, locked the door and dropped Watt's keys into a curbside rubbish can. Someone would come to look for Watt, sooner or later, and eventually they would find him with his basement cache of arms.

Or not.

It made no difference to Bolan, as he loaded the rental car with tools for the continuation of his endless war and left the neighborhood of Garnethill behind him, heading west along New City Road to Bearsden.

A slightly richer neighborhood, that was, and Bolan thought about the name while he was driving. He had no idea if there had ever been a bear in the vicinity, or if its den was anywhere nearby, but he was looking for a predator among the stylish homes that lined attractive streets, all redolent with history.

The target's name was Frankie Boyle. He'd dominated Glasgow's rackets for the past decade or so, his interests covering the normal range of gambling, prostitution, drugs, extortion, theft and loan-sharking. Through Ian Watt and several

others like him, Boyle also controlled a fair piece of illicit trafficking in arms for Glasgow and environs, which, as Bolan
understood it, covered most of Central Scotland east of Edinburgh.

It was the weapons trade that sent Bolan in search of Boyle
this afternoon. Or, more specifically, some of the people who
were purchasing his wares. A group of homegrown terrorists
whose war, though dormant for a time, had flared to life again
in recent weeks with grim results.

Bolan would happily have turned the tap to halt on illegal
weapons sales worldwide, but that would never happen, re-
alistically. One major reason was that most of the world's in-
dustrial nations—the United States included—constantly sold
guns and bombs to other countries who were ill-equipped to
make their own. Official sales were perfectly legitimate, but
once a load of hardware was delivered, the security surrounding it depended on a cast of human beings who were fallible at
best, malicious and corrupt at worst.

Add in the thefts from military arsenals and legal shipments, and you had a world armed to the teeth, with an insatia-
ble craving for more guns, more ammunition, more grenades
and rocket launchers.

Arms trafficking was the world's second-largest source
of criminal revenue, after drugs, and Bolan was a realist. He
couldn't disarm a square block in New York or Los Angeles,
much less a city the size of Glasgow. Cleaning up a state or
country? It wasn't realistic.

But he *could* stop one specific trafficker, and thereby slow
the flood of killing hardware for a day or two, until the top
man was replaced and pipelines were reopened. Bolan *could*
take out selected buyers and make sure that they never pulled
another trigger.

If his targets didn't kill him first.

Boyle's street was nice, its houses big and old enough to
rate respect. Not mansions, in the sense you might expect for
Texas oil tycoons or dot-com billionaires in Silicone Valley,

but cruising past them in a humble rented car, you knew the wealth was there.

No walled estates or obvious security devices here. Bolan drove slowly, as if looking for an address—which he was, in fact—and saw no lookouts posted on the street near number 82. No curtains flickered as he passed; why would they? he thought. Boyle would take the usual precautions: sweep the place for bugs, use prepaid cell phones for his business calls and speak in code, stash any serious incriminating items well away from his home, and pay off whichever cops would take your money and agree to drop a dime before a raid went down. Or fudge an address on a warrant, so the search was bad and anything collected would be inadmissible in court.

Friends taking care of friends.

Greed was another problem Bolan couldn't fix, and he had sworn a private vow to keep his gunsights well away from law-enforcement officers. He'd helped to put a few in prison, but if push came down to shove, there was a line he'd rather not cross.

So Glasgow's Finest, even those who weren't so very fine, had nothing to fear from Bolan. Racketeers like Frankie Boyle, however, were another story altogether.

If he'd known what was about to happen to him, to his little urban empire, Boyle would likely have been quaking in his boots. Or, maybe he was too far gone for that, a stoned psycho who never gave a second thought to fear.

Suits me, Bolan thought. Crazies died like anybody else.

He scoped the house and then drove on. Still daylight.

And the Executioner had time to kill.

2

Glasgow: 3:35 a.m.

Frankie Boyle wasn't drunk, but he was working on it. He'd been up and out since early afternoon, showing himself and being seen at the familiar haunts, checking accounts at different operations on a random basis, so the boys he'd left in charge would never know whose books might be examined next.

This night, he had surprised Joe Murray at Night Moves, one of the five strip clubs Boyle owned through paper fronts in Glasgow. One of Murray's girls—Boyle's girls, in fact—had beefed that Murray helped himself to tips beyond the standard fifty-fifty split Boyle had imposed on dancers in his joints.

That was a minor problem, which could have been resolved with just a quiet word, but Murray had been rolling certain customers, as well. Just two or three so far, but Boyle knew it would be bad for business if the word got out and customers stayed away. Worse yet, if it brought the police sniffing after Boyle.

And adding insult to the injury, Murray hadn't shared the loot he'd stolen with his boss.

Major mistake in Boyle's book.

Boyle had strolled into Night Moves at a quarter past eleven, with a couple of his boys, and put the smile on everyone in sight. He bought a round for the house and accepted the grateful applause in return, then took Murray to the soundproof office for a private chat. Murray reckoned everything was fine until he saw the ball-peen hammer, then he started bawling like a baby, blubbering and pleading innocence while Boyle got down to work.

Knuckles and walnuts sounded the same when they were crushed.

Boyle had considered smashing Murray's feet as well, but changed his mind and took the greedy bastard's shoes instead, along with keys to his brand-new Mercedes-Benz, and tossed him out the back.

Adding, "Oh, by the way, you're fecking fired," before he slammed the door.

The dancer who had tipped him off received a healthy tip and was invited to see Boyle at home after she got off work. When she'd arrived, a little after two o'clock, he'd thanked her properly. And twice more in the time since then, leaving her limp and snoring softly on his king-size bed.

No worries there, Boyle thought. He had no wife to scold him, and no kids to barge in without knocking first. After he'd satisfied his thirst, he might go back and thank the lady one more time. It would be fine if she woke up; if not, so be it.

Boyle was all about the gratitude.

Pouring his third straight double shot of Glenmorangie whisky, he thought about Murray again. In the old days, say ten years ago, he'd have likely killed the man for the money he'd stolen. Things had been tight back then, relatively, but now Boyle could dabble in mercy.

Unless Murray was stupid and tried to make trouble.

Boyle didn't mind if he stayed in Glasgow. Murray could serve as a living example of what befell those who screwed with the boss. Telling the story to selected listeners was also fine, as long as Murray was straight about it, laying out his sins. But if he started agitating, or considered talking to the filth…

Boyle sipped his whisky, savored it, deciding he could always have the boys drop Murray in the Clyde or take him

for a ride onto the moors if there were indications of his acting
up. Until then, there was no point second-guessing his original
decision.

One more shot before he went back to the dancer?

Boyle considered it, weighing the pleasure against any possible decline in his performance, and decided it was worth the
risk. These days, it took a fair amount of booze to get him
blootered, and in his opinion, he still bounced back in good
time for a man his age.

Forty and counting. Who in hell would've believed that
Frankie Boyle would last so long? he wondered.

Smiling, he took the shot glass with him. Back to thank his
friend once more, before he sent her home.

BOLAN HAD USED the day to get his bearings, gather information and to follow Frankie Boyle at a discreet distance. He'd
noted the addresses that, given the length of time Boyle spent
at them, he had to have an interest in beyond having a drink or
watching strippers work a pole.

Mapping the darker side of Glasgow, one stop at a time.

He had been parked a block away from Night Moves, south
of Bath Street, when a weeping man had lurched out of a
nearby alley, cradling hands that looked like shattered bird's
nests. Bolan let him go and wished him well if he deserved it.

Either way the man turned on Pitt Street, he would find
help waiting for him. Go south for police headquarters, north
to reach the nearest hospital ER. Both stood within a quarter mile of where Bolan had parked his rented car to wait for
Boyle's next move.

As it turned out, that was the highlight of his evening, until
he followed Boyle home and started getting ready for his unexpected meet with Glasgow's unofficial boss. The city council and police would angrily dispute that title, naturally, but
the fact remained that Boyle controlled a major portion of the
city's underground economy.

This night, that would be coming to an end.

Bolan was dressed in black street clothes with sturdy boots, and he wore a light raincoat to hide the Spectre SMG slung underneath his right arm, muzzle-heavy with its sound suppressor in place. He always came prepared for trouble. Bolan didn't know how many men Boyle had inside his great pile of a house, or how they would be armed.

Ideally, he would have a private moment with the boss and persuade Boyle to give up his terrorist contacts. But that was looking on the rosy side. Things rarely went that way for Bolan, and he guessed that Boyle would be the usual tough nut to crack.

If he had to ice the boss and squeeze somebody else, he'd do that. Ian Watt had named Boyle's number two as Erik Heriot, presumably well versed on all of Boyle's big deals. If one nut wouldn't crack…

Bolan had picked his time deliberately. Countless studies had revealed that human beings generally hit a slump at 4:00 a.m., no matter how much sleep they'd had. Reflexes lagged, distractions were routine. In hospitals, statistics showed a spike in births and deaths.

It was the Hour of the Wolf.

Or, in this case, the Hour of the Executioner.

The closest place he'd found to park was four blocks northeast of Boyle's place, but the neighborhood had alleys where the well-to-do could leave their garbage cans for pickup without ruining the trim look of their streets. Taking the back way cut his hike by half and gave Bolan a chance to come at Boyle's house from behind, instead of strolling under streetlights to the tall front door.

The backyard was surrounded by a seven-foot brick wall, but Boyle hadn't bothered to spike it or set up motion detectors. Bolan scaled the wall and lay on top of it to whistle softly, calling any dogs that might be lurking in the shadows down below, but none responded to the call. No gunmen, either, indicating that the Boss of Glasgow didn't know that he was under siege.

There had been nothing on the radio about police discovering Watt's body in the pawn shop, nothing about weapons found or anything related to them. Bolan knew police could keep things under wraps if they collaborated with the media, but unsolved homicides normally rated coverage, even if details were suppressed to weed out false confessions.

So, he had no reason to suspect that Boyle was on alert. All systems go.

Bolan rolled off the wall and dropped into darkness, landed in a crouch and struck off toward the house.

ERIK HERIOT LIT his fortieth cigarette of the day, spent close to a half-minute coughing, then expelled the smoke from his lungs with a sigh of relief. Ought to quit that, he thought, then smiled at the old game he played with himself every day.

He wasn't ready for a life change at the moment, whether it was swearing off the coffin nails, taking a pledge on booze, or looking for a so-called honest job to fill his time from nine to five.

He had one life, and this was it. He'd come a long way from the borstal time he'd served as a delinquent kid, serving these days as second in command to Frankie Boyle. Hard men all over Strathclyde knew his name, and Heriot could name a few in London who regretted crossing him.

The ones who were alive.

His life was damn near brilliant, when he thought about it, but if there was one thing he could change, it would've been the idle waiting that he had to do while Boyle had himself a frolic with a fancy bit. It was a waste of time for Heriot, in his opinion, when he could just as well be shaking down a debtor, say, or getting into some young lovely's panties himself.

Still, Heriot knew better than to bitch about it, which would certainly rebound against him. It was better if he just—

Now, what in hell was that? he thought in response to the sound he'd just heard.

It was a scuffling noise of some kind from the kitchen, he

realized. The last thing that he needed was a couple of his
boys banging the pots and pans around like Gordon Feckin'
Ramsey on the telly. If they had to scuffle, he thought, they
could do it in the yard. Or, better still, hold off until their shift
was over and go down to Rory's gym. Decide the matter in the
ring, where anyone could get a bet down and enjoy the show,
Heriot reasoned.

Fuming and trailing smoke, he made his way to the kitchen,
ready to unload on anyone who was dumb enough to start
a row inside the boss's house. He cleared the doorway and
stopped dead, surprised at seeing Billy Cutler laid out on the
floor.

His eyes were open, staring blankly at the ceiling, and what
seemed to be a bucketload of blood was pooled around his
head. He saw the gun lying next to Billy's limp right hand, and
knew there should've been the louder racket if he'd shot
himself.

So, wha—?

Warm steel made contact with his skull behind his left ear.
Heriot froze where he stood, wondering how much it would
hurt to have his brains blown out. Instead of pain and sudden
darkness, though, a voice half-whispered to him.

"Let's go see your boss," it said.

THE BACK DOOR had been unlocked for some reason. Maybe
one of Boyle's attendants had planned to take out the trash,
or perhaps it was simple negligence. Whatever the scenario, it
happened, and the ones most likely to relax their guard were
people who had been in charge so long that they'd begun to
treat the opposition with contempt.

It was a critical mistake.

Bolan had entered with the 93-R in his hand, leaving his
Spectre on its sling for the moment. The pistol left his spare
hand free for doorknobs, light switches, whatever came along
requiring manual dexterity.

He was inside, closing the door behind him, when he realized that there was someone in the pantry, off the kitchen proper to his left. Bolan was gentle with the door, but it still clicked as it was closing, and the soldier in the pantry had good ears.

"Whozat?" the man asked, and had his pistol drawn before he showed himself. Not bad, Bolan thought, risking embarrassment to hold the fort. But whoever had left the door unlocked also had signed his death warrant.

One shot from twenty feet was all it took, sinking a hole between the shooter's raised eyebrows, just a hair off center. Dying on his feet, the guy still managed two more lurching steps and fell against the stove, left arm outflung to catch the handle of a skillet, flip it once end-over-end and send it clattering across the floor as he went down.

The house was quiet, otherwise, though lights still showed in several of the windows. Bolan had to think the noise would draw somebody to investigate, and he was right. No more than thirty seconds later, when he'd nearly reached the exit to a formal dining room, he heard footsteps approaching at an urgent pace.

Bolan stepped back into a corner where the door would cover him as it was opened. Any SWAT team officer or soldier trained in urban combat would have entered in a crouch, slamming the door back to the wall and stunning anyone who might be crouched behind it, but a little racket in the kitchen didn't rate that kind of do-or-die response.

So he was ready when the new arrival entered in a cloud of cigarette smoke, gaping at the body sprawled before him. And before the second man could twitch, much less sound an alarm, Bolan had kissed his neck with the Beretta's warm suppressor.

"Let's go see your boss," he said.

The Scotsman almost nodded, then thought better of it. When he turned, it was a slow dance move, away from Bolan, waiting for the gun and whoever was holding it to go along with him. He caught the door before it closed, with his right hand, and stepped across the threshold with the same care he might exercise if he was walking on light bulbs.

"How far?" Bolan asked, not quite whispering.

"Upstairs. First floor, end of the hall."

"First floor," in the UK and most of Europe, meant what would've been the second story in the States. On this side of the water, the American first floor was called the "ground" floor, logically enough.

"You lead. Stay cool."

"As ice," his prisoner replied. Then added, "I suppose ye know yer in the shitebag now."

"You'd better hope not," Bolan told him. "If it hits the fan, you're first to go."

"Oh, aye. Ah figgered that."

They'd reached the stairs, and Bolan's captive started up them, taking each step with leaden strides.

"Faster," Bolan instructed.

"Och, I wouldn't wanna get me arse shot off fer runnin', now."

Before Bolan could answer, two men suddenly appeared above him, on the first-floor landing. Both scowled down at him, then reached for pistols tucked into their belts. He reached around his hostage, winged the shooter on his right.

And then all hell broke loose.

FRANKIE BOYLE was half asleep when sounds of gunfire yanked him back to consciousness. He tumbled out of bed, naked, his first instinct being to save himself if shooters were about to crash his bedroom door. Another second told him that the noise was buffered by a few more walls, which he figured meant he had at least a little time.

Job one: retrieve the Browning Hi-Power semiauto pistol from the top drawer of his nightstand and be ready to defend himself.

Job two: while covering the door, hit speed-dial on his cell phone for his houseman, to find out exactly what in bloody hell was happening.

Job three: put on some clothes.

The woman from Night Moves had begun to squeal and wouldn't shut it when he snapped at her, so Boyle reached up and banjoed her with the 9 mm pistol. He thought he heard her nose crack, but had no time to consider it.

The phone rang three times and was going into number four when houseman Davey Bryce answered, breathless. "Yeah?"

"What's all the feckin' racket, then?" Boyle demanded.

"Someone's got inside. I dunno—"

And the line went dead.

Boyle squeezed and shook the cell phone, all in vain. He thumbed redial, waited forever, just to hear a robo-voice say that his party wasn't answering.

"No shite!" he snarled, and disconnected. He pressed another button with his thumb and waited through two rings before a gruff voice answered.

"Yeah, so?"

"Is ya feckin' deaf or what, then? We're gettin' shot to tatters while you're whackin' off. Get yer ass over here right now!"

Boyle cut the link without waiting for a response and scrambled toward the nearby closet on his hands and knees. His private dancer was still wailing from the bed, likely to bring the home invaders down on top of them unless she shut it, but he couldn't bring himself to shoot her.

Not in his own bed.

Boyle reached the walk-in closet, crawled inside and only then stood up. For all he knew, a bullet might come punching through one of the walls and find him there, but he felt safer, anyway.

And he still had a wild card up his sleeve.

The neighbors didn't know—or else, pretended not to—that he owned *two* houses on their precious tree-lined street. One that he lived and partied in, and one next door, immediately to the north, where shooters slept in shifts, ready to scramble in a heartbeat if their boss was threatened. Boyle had built a gate into the fence that separated his two properties, so troops could pass without alerting any watchers on the street.

Not that he gave a damn for stealth tonight, though, with some bastard shooting up his house. His neighbors would be calling up the police by now, he thought. Boyle only hoped that he could meet one of the bastards face-to-face, before the police rolled in.

And maybe get the hell away from there, as well.

But just in case, once Boyle had pulled his trousers on, he made another call. To his solicitor, this time. He figured that for what he charged per hour, the old prick could damn well haul his fat ass out of bed and meet Boyle at the lockup.

Just in case.

FOR SIX OR SEVEN seconds, there was chaos on the staircase. Bolan's first shot clipped one shooter's left biceps and staggered him, but both of Boyle's men still had their guns in hand an instant later, unloading in rapid-fire. Bolan hunched down behind his human shield, felt the man taking some hits while other bullets sizzled past him, then returned fire with his autoloader set for 3-round bursts.

The wounded gunner took a round in the upper chest and sat down hard, then toppled forward, tumbling down the stairs in jerky somersaults. His partner tried retreating, nearly lost his balance with a misstep, throwing out one hand to catch himself. Before he could recover, Bolan's Parabellum rounds sheared off the right side of his face and sprayed the wall behind him with gray matter.

Done.

Bolan charged up the stairs, taking three at a time, hoping he'd find the first-floor hallway clear between himself and Boyle. He needed time to squeeze the boss and get the information he required, before police came rolling in to spoil the probe.

And failing that…then, what?

No sirens, but he heard a crash downstairs as someone forced a door, then half-a-dozen voices, maybe more, were clamoring for Boyle, advancing toward the stairs. None of the new arrivals bothered to identify themselves as cops, and when he glanced over the railing, Bolan saw that they were reinforcements for the home team, closing in to help the man who signed their paychecks.

Say a dozen guns down there, at least, he figured. Where had they come from? He didn't know and didn't care. Only the fact of their existence mattered, and the weapons in their hands.

One of them fired a shotgun blast at Bolan, shattering the banister as he ducked back and out of sight. More bullets followed, peppering the walls and ceiling overhead. Retreating, he could see the door to Frankie Boyle's bedroom, but Bolan knew the room could be a death trap. Boyle could pin him on the threshold, while his men came up behind and finished Bolan with a spray of lead.

Forget it.

Barging through the first door on his right, he found himself inside what he supposed had to be a guest room, with a queen-sized bed immediately to his left, an en suite to his right. Directly opposite the doorway where he stood, a sliding window faced the yard and street beyond across a narrow balcony.

Call it a drop of twenty feet, and then a run of twenty yards or so across the gently sloping lawn, wide open to Boyle's shooters in the house and any who were quick enough to follow him. Bolan would still be four blocks from his car, and he wasn't sure that he could risk running directly to it, with a pack of gunmen on his heels.

So, take it one step at a time.

Bolan kicked the bedroom door shut, latched it, then crossed to the window. He opened that and hesitated, waiting for the sound of angry voices to resume from the hallway. If

they went straight for Boyle, he had a chance to make the drop
unnoticed. If they started searching room by room...

The doorknob jiggled, and he stitched a double 3-round
burst across the paneling, rewarded with a squeal of pain. A
second later, he was on the balcony, one leg across the rail,
as small-arms fire ripped through the guest room's door and
eastern wall. Artwork exploded, tumbling, and the furniture
was taking hits as Bolan made his leap of faith.

He landed in a crouch and rolled once, bouncing to his feet
as he came out of it. He sprinted for the sidewalk on a long
diagonal, trying to gain ground in the general direction of his
rental car while he had a chance. Hurdling a low fence meant
to keep trespassers off the grass, he hit the sidewalk running,
as a low-slung car roared up and swung in to the curb.

His piece was up and tracking toward the driver's face and
locked there, as the woman at the wheel asked him, "Care for
a lift?"

3

Washington, D.C., two days earlier

Parking was easier in Washington the farther you got from the White House. Not *easy,* but *easier,* as in, you only had to drive around the block four or five times for a space with marginal security.

Bolan motored north on Sixteenth Street, leaving the monuments and barricades behind, letting the flow of morning traffic carry him along. Most people who had jobs would be at work by this time. But Washington was not only the capital of paper shuffling, but also of people on the move: between office blocks, en route to courthouses and libraries; filing writs and motions; carrying messages that couldn't be trusted to phones or encrypted e-mails.

The soldier avoided Washington—or Wonderland, as he had learned to think of it during his long and lonely war against the Mafia—whenever possible. He had no business there, per se, since he did not officially exist. His death in New York City was a matter of public record, literally carved in stone.

How often did a soldier get to visit his own grave?

Still, Hal Brognola worked in Washington, at the Justice Department's headquarters on Pennsylvania Avenue. There were times he couldn't get away to Stony Man Farm in Virginia for a face-to-face with Bolan, and on those occasions the

Executioner used his knowledge of the teeming city's streets to good advantage.

On this day, they were meeting at a new spot: the Supreme Council of the Scottish Rite of Freemasonry, in the 1700 block of 16th Street, Northwest. Bolan wasn't a member of the lodge, and he had never seen Brognola sporting a Masonic ring, but he assumed that the big Fed had chosen the location for a reason that would soon become apparent.

Meanwhile, Bolan had done his homework online. He knew that the Scottish Rite branch of Freemasonry had been founded in Charleston, South Carolina, in 1801. Its best-known promoter and primary architect of lodge ritual was Albert Pike, a Boston native who moved south and later wound up fighting as a Confederate brigadier general in the Civil War. Some conspiracy theorists named Pike as a founder of the original Ku Klux Klan, but most historians dismissed that claim as false.

Beyond that, Bolan knew the lodge had thirty-three "degrees" of membership, with titles advancing from "master traveler" to "inspector general" at the pyramid's apex. Much of the lodge's dogma was cloaked in secrecy, but its public face included extensive work on behalf of dyslexic children and maintenance of two first-rate pediatric hospitals, in Dallas and Atlanta.

Bolan reached his destination—an imposing edifice known as the House of the Temple—and motored past in search of available parking. He found it two blocks farther north, pulled his ticket out of a machine and walked back in the warm sunshine.

He already knew that the House of the Temple was open for tours between 10:00 a.m. and 4:00 p.m., September through February.

Bolan had a jump on some of the other tourists approaching the House of the Temple that morning. He'd already taken a "virtual tour" of the complex, and so knew what to expect. Steps rising in groups of three, five, seven and nine brought him to the main entrance: a bronze door flanked by two lime-stone sphinxes and thirty-three columns, each thirty-three feet tall. The sphinx to the right of the door had its eyes half-open, symbolizing wisdom, while its partner was wide-eyed, representing power.

The soldier entered through the tall polished doors, passing into an atrium that served as the central court of the temple. He had exact change ready for the ticket, palmed it and scanned the spacious chamber with its marble floor and benches, eight huge Doric columns carved from granite and bronze plaques on the walls displaying various Masonic symbols. Overhead, bronze chandeliers with alabaster bowls provided light.

Bolan drifted toward the central feature of the atrium, a table wrought from Italian marble, supported by double-headed eagles that served as the lodge's insignia. From the temple's website, he knew that the Latin inscription—*Salve Frater*—translated into English as "Welcome Brother."

Bolan had nearly reached the table when a gruff, familiar voice behind him said, "You're right on time."

HAL BROGNOLA LOOKED the same as always, stylish in a rumpled sort of way, frowning a little, as if carrying a load of worry on his shoulders. Which, on any given day, he was.

Each time they met, Bolan wondered about the secrets locked inside Brognola's head: the threats that he'd been called upon to deal with, orders he had issued in response, the missions he'd directed that would place good men and women in harm's way. They only talked about the jobs he had for Bolan, but the story didn't end there. Never had, and never would, as long as Brognola stayed at his post.

"I aim for punctuality," Bolan replied to the big Fed's remark.

"And always were a marksman." As they shook hands, Brognola said, "I suppose you're wondering about this place."

"I did some research on the internet," Bolan said. "Nothing too mysterious, except your choice of meeting places."

"I was going for a theme," he said. "Let's walk."

They passed a pair of Egyptian-style statues inscribed with hieroglyphs. From his virtual tour, Bolan knew they were carved out of marble quarried at Lake Champlain, New York. The inscriptions referred to wise men and the glory of God.

"It's not about the Masons," Brognola advised him.

"I didn't think it was."

"But I was in a Scottish state of mind."

"Okay." He waited for Brognola to spill it in his own good time.

They left the atrium behind, to enter the temple's executive chamber. The grand commander's throne sat facing the doorway, under a plush canopy, while thirty-three empty chairs awaited members of the supreme council. A gold-inlaid ceiling topped heavy plaster walls with intricate accents of black leaves and vines, with dark walnut woodwork throughout.

"You heard about the incident last week in Glasgow?" Brognola inquired.

"The basics," Bolan said. "Ground breaking for a factory. Somebody shot it up and killed the CEO, along with others."

"Which includes an unarmed cop," Brognola said. "Long story short, the shooters got away, but they claimed credit."

"Oh?"

"That only made the local news, maybe a blurb in London. Nothing to compete with talk-show crap and Jersey-liquor nonsense over here."

"Who pulled it off?" Bolan asked.

"It's a homegrown outfit called the Tartan Independence Front," Brognola said. "Some kind of spin-off from the Tartan Army, if you still remember them."

"It rings a bell," Bolan replied.

One corner of Brognola's mouth twitched with the bare suggestion of a smile. "Word is, they didn't want to sound like copycats, so when they started up, they called their gang the

Scottish Independence Front. But changed it pretty quickly, when they got wind of the reaction to their tagged initials."

"SIF?" Bolan said. "I imagine so."

"What self-respecting revolutionary wants to be confused with a disease?" Brognola asked.

Climbing marble stairs to reach the temple's banquet hall, they reached the middle landing and paused to admire the Pillars of Charity alcove, a "light well" of stained glass framed by bronze. The pillars themselves were jet-black and polished to a mirror shine.

"So, you've got Scotsmen mad at England," Bolan said. "What else is new?"

"This isn't *Braveheart* or *Rob Roy*," Brognola said. "Try Baader-Meinhof in a kilt and tam-o'-shanter."

Bolan almost laughed aloud at that, but caught himself in time. "Okay," he said. "It sounds like something for SO15."

Meaning the former Special Branch of Scotland Yard, which had merged with the Metropolitan Police Anti-Terrorist Branch in 2006, to create a new Counter Terrorism Command. The "SO" stood for Special Operations. Where they got the "15" would be anybody's guess, Bolan thought.

"It would be," Brognola replied, "but we've got pressure over here because the latest victim was American."

"One of the victims," Bolan said.

"You're right. But he was rich and influential, with at least a dozen friends in Congress, one of them a senator."

"All squeaky wheels," Bolan said.

"And yours truly is expected to supply the grease," he said.

"Won't the locals be all over it?" Bolan asked.

"Locals, officials from London, they may even call in some talent from MI5 and the SIS."

Britain's Security Service and Secret Intelligence Service.

"Sounds like I'd have more badges on my hands than terrorists," Bolan observed.

"You'd have to watch your step," Brognola said, "but I think it's doable."

"Why don't you drop the other shoe," Bolan suggested.

"Damn. Was I that obvious?"

"If this was just about a CEO and pacifying congressmen, Justice would send an FBI team out to help the Brits."

"They're doing that," Brognola said.

"More badges. Great. Let's hear the rest."

They'd reached the temple's library, billed as the oldest open to the public in D.C. There were a quarter of a million books on hand, including some printed by Benjamin Franklin a decade before the American Revolution.

"The TIF is marginal," Brognola said. "Maybe a thousand members total. But they're getting cash and arms from somewhere, out of all proportion to their size and overall importance in the scheme of things."

"What are you thinking? Eastern Europe? China?"

"Possibly," Brognola answered. "But it feels closer to home. The guns aren't hard to find. The cash…that's something else."

"So, I'd be looking for the source."

Brognola took a CD from an inside pocket of his tailored coat and handed it to Bolan.

"Have a look at this," he said, "and tell me when you're good to go."

BOLAN CHECKED into a Days Inn on the Clara Barton Parkway, near Glen Echo Park in Maryland. He took a single room, no frills, and didn't bother to unpack. Set up his laptop on the rooms lone table, by a window facing the parking lot, and slipped Brognola's disk into the CD drive. He opened its single file, then cracked a soda from the minibar and settled down to read.

The Tartan Independence Front had organized five years earlier, based on the information gleaned by Scotland Yard from interviews, wiretaps and other sources. Its founders were admirers—some said ex-members—of the old Tartan Army, a group supporting Scottish independence from the UK that had carried out a string of bombings and other terrorist acts from the early 1970s until a mass roundup and trial of identified members twenty years later. Despite their best efforts, they'd never come close to rivaling the IRA.

But it seemed that someone was ready to try again.

The TIF's supposed leader was Fergus Gibson, an Edinburgh native born in 1976, whose father had been implicated in—but never charged with—one of the Tartan Army's bombings in Manchester, England. Examining his face in photographs, Bolan supposed that maybe rebellion ran in the blood. There was a set to Gibson's jaw, a frown that seemed to be perpetual. Or was it simply that surveillance photos had been snapped when he was in a dour mood?

Gibson had finished three semesters at Edinburgh Napier University before dropping out, without explanation, at age twenty. While it lasted, he'd majored in engineering. His employment record showed stints as a trucker, construction worker and operator of heavy equipment. As far as anyone could tell, he'd never voted in his life, and never voiced any political opinions prior to cofounding the TIF with the guy who reportedly served as his second in command.

Graham Wallace was a year older than Gibson, but there was no indication that he'd ever tried to run the show. A Highlander from Inverness, he'd never been to college but had gone the hard-knocks route, including multiple encounters with the justice system. Five arrests were on record, two of which resulted in convictions. Wallace had served nine months at HM Prison Aberdeen for assaulting a policeman, followed by two-and-a-half years at HM Prison Barlinnie for second-degree arson. The target in that case had been a police car. Intoxication and a psych exam had dropped the charge from first degree.

Since its inception, the TIF had been linked to bombings in Glasgow, Edinburgh, Abderdeen, Dundee and Inverness. Each blast—and two bombs that failed to explode, in Aberfoyle and Lockerbie—had targeted shops or factories owned by English investors. Recently, suspected TIF bombers had left their home turf to detonate charges in Manchester, Leeds, York and London. None of the attacks had claimed a life.

Until Glasgow.

The TIF—if it had done the Lockhart job, which Bolan had no cause to doubt—was stepping up its game. Warnings were out; bloodshed was in. And if Brognola was correct, which normally turned out to be the case, the new aggressive attitude was being fueled by fresh infusions of cash, source unknown.

There'd been a time when Bolan would have looked to Moscow first, but Russia was a mess these days, nearly bankrupt, ruled by a decadent kleptocracy that was too busy stealing to foment some crackpot revolution in the West. The Russians might sell guns to Gibson and his crew, but the days of free hardware and lavish donations to leftist guerrillas were gone.

Who else was in the business of supporting terrorism? China focused mainly on the Far East, and was having trouble with its homegrown dissidents, as well as agitation over the long-running occupation of Tibet. Cuban agents kept their hands in with Latin American activists and some outposts in Africa, but Europe had proved to be sterile ground for Castro-style radicalism.

That left the Middle East, but terror's financiers in that region generally confined their support to Islamic extremists, or at least to die-hard enemies of Israel. Iran, Syria and Saudi Arabia had no more in common with the TIF than with the IRA in Belfast or the Ku Klux Klan in the United States.

Call it a mystery. It wouldn't be the first Bolan had cracked by application of strategic pressure. And, with any luck, it wouldn't be the last.

With the critical information committed to memory, Bolan hit the CD's drop-down menu and ordered his laptop to Erase This Disk. It took about a minute, then he double-checked, extracted the CD, snapped it in two and dropped it in the small trash can beside him.

Done.

Bolan booked his flight from JFK to Glasgow International online, showered, set his alarm for 6:00 a.m. and went to sleep.

AFTER AN EARLY breakfast at the motel's coffee shop, Bolan drove north from Washington to Newark, New Jersey, arriving just after 10:30 a.m., with six hours left before check-in at JFK.

By 11:15 a.m., Bolan was crossing the Goethals Bridge to pick up the Staten Island Expressway, making good time heading toward Brooklyn where he'd drop the rental car.

Ace Storage stood on Flatbush Avenue, between Marine Park and Floyd Bennett Field. A cyclone fence topped with razor wire surrounded ten ranks of fifty storage units each, which rented by the month or year. Bolan's was number 319, secured with a combination lock that packed a two-gram high-explosive wallop if you failed to get the numbers lined up properly in two attempts.

Bolan had similar facilities across the country in various places. Each held weapons, ammunition and assorted other items that might be of use to him in an emergency. The rental fees were paid by credit card, through Stony Man, on active accounts maintained under half a dozen false names. Each straw man had a Grade-A credit rating. None appeared in any law-enforcement registry or other database maintained by state or federal government. Their addresses were local mail drops, but the bills were paid online. If anybody stole one of the bills and tried to scam the card's owner—which hadn't happened yet—the consequences would be suitably severe.

Bolan spent fifteen minutes in his storage unit on the early afternoon of his departure from the States. He left behind one of his four Beretta 93-R pistols, with its shoulder harness, and an MP-5 K submachine gun that he'd kept beneath the hired car's shotgun seat. Also abandoned for the moment was a Gerber automatic knife with four-inch tanto blade, serrated over half its cutting edge—a modern switchblade, in effect.

Opening a compact fireproof safe, Bolan removed a passport, California driver's license, credit cards and other basic ID matching the "Matthew Cooper" name on his flight reservation. Name and address aside, the items were legitimate, concocted from originals secured through Brognola's Stony Man team. The phone number displayed on Cooper's driver's license would ring through a relay in Los Angeles, to a voice-mail system at Stony Man Farm, in Virginia. Bolan, as Cooper, could check his messages from anywhere on Earth, but didn't have to answer.

After all, he was on vacation.

It was a short drive from Ace Storage to JFK International Airport via Shore Parkway and the Nassau Expressway. He dropped his rental car at 1:05 p.m., ate an overpriced lunch in Terminal 4, and took his time checking in for his 6:30 p.m. flight. Security was slow, as always, with the standard questions, pat downs, and inspections of a thousand shoes.

Bolan passed through the metal detector, raised his arms for an up-and-down pass with a handheld security wand, then waited for his shoes and carry-on to clear the X-ray machine. No weapons there, and nothing to excite the watchers even if they sought a closer look, but he was passed on without opening his bag.

The rest came down to waiting at the designated gate until his flight was called, reading a travel guide to Scotland that he bought at Hudson News. A detailed map of Glasgow was included.

By the time a disembodied voice announced the start of boarding for his flight, Bolan was more than ready to be on his way. A patient man by any standard, trained to lie in wait for days behind a sniper scope if need be, he still chafed inside at the inevitable downtime between his acceptance of a mission and the moment when he hit the ground running, embarking on yet another gamble with the Reaper.

Every time he took a job from Brognola, his life was on the line. Bolan accepted that, but didn't like to sit around and think about it, when he could be taking action to resolve the issue on his own terms, carrying the battle to his enemies.

Rising to shuffle forward with the other passengers, when his row was called to board, Bolan looked forward to an opportunity for sleeping on the flight. Once he arrived, there might be no rest until he was finished with his job.

Or until the job had finished him.

The thought was there and gone, dismissed as unproductive and defeatist. Bolan always planned to win and to survive. Someday, when he ran out of time like every other human on the planet, he would meet his fate with eyes wide open, fighting back against the darkness.

And he damn sure wouldn't go alone.

4

Glasgow: Present day, 4:36 a.m.

Bolan had a split second to consider his options, peering at the redhead belted in behind the wheel of a tiny Ford Ka that looked as if it had been kicked in the back end by a giant. He could either squeeze into the shotgun seat, or run for it and hope Boyle's shooters lost him in the dark.

He squeezed, she nodded and the little car peeled out with squealing tires.

"We won't have long," she said, working the clutch and five-speed shift as if she knew her way around a race track.

Bolan checked his wing mirror and saw that she was right. Headlights were lancing out of Boyle's driveway and swinging after them in hot pursuit. Just one car followed them, likely with three to five men packed inside it, while the rest scrambled to clean up Frankie's house before the law arrived.

"You always pick up strangers in the middle of a firefight?" Bolan asked her, cutting to the other chase.

"Depends," she answered with an unexpected smile. "Call it a whim."

"Whims can be dangerous," he said.

"You plan to shoot me, then?"

"Depends," he echoed her. "I have to see whose side you're on."

"My own," she said. "How's that?"

"It doesn't tell me much," Bolan replied.

"Call it a spin on the old fable, then," she said. "This time, the damsel saves the bad man in distress."

He flicked another glance at the wing mirror and said, "It works for me, except they're breathing down our necks right now."

"'O ye of little faith,'" she said, and smiled again, shifting the Ka's transmission into fifth for greater speed.

That gave the little car a boost, but they could only go so fast with the Duratec 1.6-liter engine under its hood. They had some kind of full-sized muscle car pursuing them, its occupants likely prepared to open fire as soon as they were close enough to aim reliably, and Bolan didn't have to ask if there was any body armor on the Ka.

"Hang on!" his savior warned, downshifting half a second later as they snarled into a sudden left-hand turn. She clearly meant to prove that what her compact lacked in power, it made up in handling.

Bolan clenched his teeth, hung on and wished her well. He thought about his safety harness, just in case they hit something or someone, but decided not to use it. If they had to stop and fight, he didn't want to waste an extra microsecond fumbling with an unfamiliar seat belt, when he could be sighting on his would-be killers with the Spectre SMG.

Bolan was simultaneously checking out the street in front of them, watching the mirror, thinking through the moves he'd have to make if they were stopped, and watching out for landmarks to stay oriented with the street map he had memorized. He knew they were headed north when he got in the Ka, then west after the first turn, but it started getting hectic after that. They stayed with residential streets, but Bolan thought that they were headed in the general direction of the River Clyde.

For what? Hoping to lose their trackers in a maze of byways? Or to find a place where they could stand and fight?

He took a closer look at the woman who had rescued him. Her face was set in grim determination, and if he had to guess, he'd say that she was every inch a pro.

So much for whimsy and coincidence.

Bolan had to ask himself what kind of pro she was, who she was working for, and how she'd happened to be passing Frankie Boyle's house at the very moment when he needed help.

If help was even what she had in mind.

Forget about the smile that could disguise a plan to kill him. But if that was all she wanted, why play out the whole charade to start with? She could just as easily have shot him on the street—or spared herself the whole routine by letting Boyle's men do the dirty work. And would a gutter thug like Boyle even have a female hitter on his crew?

Unlikely, but it wouldn't be the strangest thing the Executioner had seen.

Not by a long kill shot.

Wondering if he would have to kill the woman while they sped along at sixty-something miles per hour in her little clown car, thinking that the crash would likely kill him, Bolan watched his mirror, watched her hands and watched the road, hoping his wild ride through the night was nearly done.

"THERE'S TWO OF 'EM," Des Buchan said, pushing the BMW 3 Series Saloon to catch the fleeing midget car.

"Ya reckon? I thought it was drivin' by itsel'," Roddy Lauder said, laying on the scorn.

His driver winced. Started to say, "I just meant—"

"Shoosh and watch the feckin' road, will ya?" To the others, in the backseat, Lauder snapped, "And have your shooters ready!"

Graeme Godley and Harry Baxter didn't answer. They knew better than to question Lauder when he was in a foul mood, and the job was simple anyhow. Run down the gunner who had shot up Boyle's place, along with whoever had plucked him off the street outside, and do them proper. Boyle hadn't asked for tokens this time, since the cops would be in every nook and cranny any minute, but Lauder knew there was a camera in the BMW's glove box he could use to snap some pictures when they'd finished.

Something for the old scrapbook.

The fella they were chasing had an automatic weapon, and it wouldn't do to overlook the driver at a time like this. Say one more gun, at least, and even with the odds at two-to-one against them, they were dangerous. Just look at what the one alone had done to Boyle's bodyguards before the reinforcements sorted him.

Except, they *hadn't* sorted him, had they? No. They'd let him skip.

An error Roddy Lauder and his boys were duty-bound to fix before they showed their faces around the boss again.

Should be no problem there, with the equipment they were packing. Lauder had a Mossberg pump-action shotgun cut down to basics, loaded with six rounds of No. 1 buckshot and his pockets rattling with spares. His backup was a SIG-Sauer P-239 chambered in .357 SIG, because he liked the kick and bang.

Godley and Baxter both had TEC-9 pistols from the States that had been modified to fire full-automatic by a Glasgow gunsmith, after Boyle bought a shipment of them from a fella who was cozy with the mafia in New York. Cheaper than MAC-10s by a long chalk, they could unload their thirty-two rounds in a couple of seconds and nail any bastard unlucky enough to be standing downrange.

Des Buchan had only a pistol, he knew, but it was a corker, an Israeli Desert Eagle that weighed in around five pounds when it was loaded, and no wonder Des was always bitching about problems with his back, the way his holster dragged one shoulder out of line. Lauder had seen him shoot the damn thing once, and reckoned it could knock the little Ka that they were chasing off the bloody road, all by itself.

But all the hardware in the world wouldn't accomplish anything unless they caught the intruders they were chasing. Going back to Boyle empty-handed wasn't an option. In fact, they might as well just park the BMW and shoot one another if they couldn't bag their men.

Boyle wouldn't let them off that easy, if they failed.

"Faster!" he snapped at Buchan. "You're drivin' like a scaredy-cat."

"The hell!" Buchan answered, but he put it on the floor and milked a few more miles per hour from the racing engine.

"Makin' for the Clyde, are they?" Godley asked from the back.

"I don't know what they're thinkin'," Lauder said. "Just catch 'em, right quick!"

"This thing don't fly," Buchan answered back.

"Maybe we need another pilot, then."

That brought a muttered curse and yet another burst of speed, closing the gap between their BMW and the Ka. He had to give the other driver credit, though, for whipping turns each time they gained a bit.

Wherever they were running to, Lauder was sticking to them to the bloody end.

And bloody it would damn well be.

THE KA WHIPPED through another squealing turn, and when they straightened out again Bolan inquired, "Is there a destination in our future?"

"Almost there," the lady said.

He didn't press it. Shifting slightly in his seat, the soldier kept the Spectre's muzzle pointed at the floorboard but relaxed his right knee, clearing up his field of fire. He'd turned the SMG around for left-hand firing when he got into the car, accommodating the realities of right-hand drive, but still hoped that he wouldn't have to kill the woman where she sat. Bolan recalled the first time he'd been forced to stop a female killer with a bullet, half a world away from where he sat, and in another lifetime. If he never had to make that choice again, it would be too damned soon.

So he hung on and waited, checking out the chase car's

progress in his mirror, making sure the redhead didn't let her hands stray from the steering wheel and gearshift. If she reached under her jacket, or went groping for her bag...

"And here we are," she said. But showed no sign of slowing, much less stopping, as they made another turn and roared into a short block lined with fish markets and smallish seafood restaurants.

Some kind of wharf lay dead ahead, and for a second Bolan thought she meant to drive out there, the riverside equivalent of a box canyon, but the Ka's headlights revealed a pair of heavy metal stanchions that blocked vehicle access to the pier.

Instead of charging straight ahead, the woman cut another sharp right-hand turn and raced along the riverfront for about a hundred yards. There were a few boats moored on Bolan's side, all dark and seemingly deserted, but he concentrated on his mirror and saw headlights coming after them again, switching to high beams.

The shooters wanted light to work by when they opened up.

Two hundred yards ahead, Bolan saw empty darkness and assumed that they were running out of road. He didn't know if it would mean another right-hand turn, putting the river at their backs and running back toward town, or if the option was a launch into black water. Bolan didn't fancy going for a swim, and flicked a leftward glance to verify that he could reach the handle on his door, and that it was still unlocked.

"Don't worry," the lady said. "I'm not taking you to feed the water kelpies."

"Good to know," Bolan replied, without a clue to what she meant.

"I'd hoped to lose them, but they're sticky," she continued. "Are you halfway decent with that shooter?"

"Halfway," he allowed.

"Let's see, then."

As she spoke, the redhead revved the engine, then slammed on the brake and spun her steering wheel hard to the left. The Ka spun through a dizzying 180, various components making noises they were never meant to utter, and the car wound up facing back the way they'd come, with the chase car's high beams glaring into Bolan's face.

"Best to get out now," she advised him, sounding almost casual about it. "Just in case they ram us."

She took time to loop the long strap of her purse over a shoulder, while she drew a semiauto pistol from a holster Bolan hadn't seen. He made it for a Glock, but couldn't guess the caliber or model as she bailed out of the Ka.

Bolan had no bag to retrieve, but thought about his other hardware in the hired car he had left behind. Some of it might have come in handy, but it was far beyond his reach. There was a chance he'd never get it back, even if he survived the next few minutes, but he put that out of mind and focused on the task at hand.

Survival.

The Spectre's maximum effective range was listed as one hundred yards, and while the weapon's Parabellum rounds could kill beyond that distance, no one in his or her right mind ever tried to score hits with an SMG over the full length of a football field. Cut that by half, and you'd be lucky if one bullet from a 12-round burst did any lasting damage to a man-sized target. Submachine guns were intended to fire pistol ammunition, and most shoot-outs using handguns happened at a range of thirty feet or less.

So Bolan waited, crouched behind a handy garbage bin, tracking with the gun's iron sights. The high beams couldn't blind him from here, unless the speeding car swerved toward his hiding place. In which case he had bigger problems than the glare of headlights.

Fifty feet and closing. Almost there.

He heard the redhead's pistol crack, a classic double-tap, and still he waited. Gave them five more yards, imagining the driver's face behind that tinted windshield glass, before he let the Spectre rip.

"THEY'RE DONE NOW," Des Buchan said, and cackled with delight.

"They're not done if they're breathin'," Roddy Lauder contradicted him. "Just get us there, an' don't go smashin' into their toy car."

He thumbed off the Mossberg's safety and powered down his window, just in case he got a chance to pot one of the people he was gunning for off to the riverside. It had surprised him when the car that they'd been chasing made a racing turn and faced back toward them, then stopped dead, its driver and the shooter bailing out, but he supposed they'd seen the writing on the wall.

Nowhere to run, but they could still peel off and try to hide.

That made it awkward, with the warehouses along the riverfront. They could be all night checking shadows, looking for the pricks who'd shot up Boyle's house, and Lauder knew that workmen started showing up along the river prior to sunrise. Still, his orders had been clear. He couldn't go back to the boss without a pair of scalps to show for it.

He was about to caution Buchan, tell him to slow it down, when muzzle-flashes winked in front of them on either side, and someone hit the windshield with a sledgehammer. Buchan made a raspy hawking sound, as something warm and wet spattered the right-hand side of Lauder's face. The salty taste of blood was in his mouth and nearly made him gag, recoiling from the faceless corpse beside him, in the BMW's driver's seat.

"Jaysus!" someone behind him blurted, maybe Graeme Godley, then the BMW swerved off to the left, with one of Buchan's arms stuck through the steering wheel, his weight dragging it over as he slumped toward Lauder, spilling blood and muck.

"Jump clear!" Lauder barked, clawing at his door handle, hoping Baxter and Godley had the sense to bail before Buchan ran them off the dock and out into the Clyde. Somehow, he kept the Mossberg as he tumbled from the car, wrenching his shoulder on impact and cursing at the pain.

Baxter struck pavement several yards beyond, while Lauder lurched and staggered to his feet. He heard the other man's TEC-9 clatter on the blacktop, Baxter bleating, then it was a rush to find the nearest cover he could manage before someone cut him down. Every man for himself, and the devil take the hindmost.

Still, he had to pause and glance back when he heard the BMW strike some solid object, crunching in the bumper and the grille. Against all odds, it hadn't gone into the drink, but hit one of the tall, tarred posts that marked the river's edge where boats were moored. Lauder had time to see Godley leap out of the car, running almost before his feet touched down, then gunfire crackled from the shadows and he dived headlong behind a steel cargo container streaked with rust.

Not perfect, but the bullets couldn't reach him there, until the shooters moved around to get a better angle on him. In the meantime, Lauder heard one of the friendly TEC-9s stutter, helping to distract the enemy and maybe even score a fluky hit, if he was lucky.

Embarrassed at hiding and anxious to get in the fight, Lauder clutched his shotgun in a white-knuckle grip and edged forward, crouching for another moment in relative safety and steeling his nerve before he leaned out for a look at the battleground.

Nothing in sight from that point, but he counted the flashes from four different guns, knew his boys were still in it and raring to go. If he didn't jump in pretty soon, they'd be spreading the story all over by this time tomorrow. Or else they'd be dead, and him with them.

No choice, then.

In brawls, sometimes, Lauder would cow his opposition with a roaring battle cry, but this occasion called for something else entirely. Godley and Baxter had the opponents distracted for the moment, giving him a chance to pull a stealth maneuver and come out a hero, if he didn't muck it up.

Lauder swallowed a humbling dose of fear and broke from cover, sprinting over open pavement toward the south side of Dockland Street.

BOLAN HAD HOPED to see the chase car take a nosedive, but the crew got lucky with a dead man at the wheel. Once they were out and under cover, more or less, it turned into a game of cat and mouse, with both sides trying hard to play the cat.

The odds weren't bad, at three-to-two, but he was worried about time. Even with the apparently deserted riverfront, it wouldn't be much longer before early birds began reporting to their jobs, and that would mean a rash of phone calls to the Strathclyde cops who covered Glasgow and eleven other council districts stretching from the west coast to the Southern Uplands. Most of them were too far distant to respond, but several hundred could be scrambled in emergencies.

And any duel with automatic weapons would be rated top priority.

He couldn't speak for the redhead who'd brought him there, but Bolan didn't plan on meeting any cops on this night—or any other time, if he could help it. That meant taking out the hunters in a hurry and departing from the scene before the first squad cars rolled in.

He got lucky with the first one. He had begun to shift positions when a lanky shooter with some kind of small machine pistol broke cover, running zigzag over open ground and firing as he came.

Bolan could only guess what motivated him and didn't really care. His Spectre spit a 5-round burst that dropped the runner on his face. The dead or dying shooter slid for several yards, then came to rest with curly hair butted against a curb.

The odds were even.

Bolan moved on, circled around the garbage bin and kept going, stalking with the broad bulk of a warehouse at his back.

Another light machine pistol was spitting rounds toward the place where he'd been crouching when he shot the careless gunman, and he marked the muzzle-flash, refrained from firing until he could close the gap a little more.

It didn't have to be a perfect shot, of course. He still had thirty-something rounds left in his weapon's casket magazine, with two spares waiting, but he didn't like to waste good ammunition. If he got a little closer, just a few more steps...

Off to his right, a blur of movement told him where the redhead was, suddenly exposed, either seeking to improve her cover or obtain a better angle on the fight. He hoped she wouldn't die before he found out who she was and why she'd helped him, but he couldn't help her at the moment.

Unless he dropped the shooter who was tracking her.

Across the street, his target opened fire, 9 mm bullets rattling off downrange. Bolan was ready with the Spectre, hammering a burst into the guy before his target had a chance to recognize his fatal error.

Which left one.

But where was he?

There were two ways to go. Hunt the lone survivor down, or head back to the Ka and hope he'd let them go, knowing the odds had turned against him. They'd be easy marks, retreating, and a car was always easier to hit than individuals on foot. Still, if they hung around to root him out, the fourth man could escape and they would never know it, rooting through the shadows until prowl cars had them boxed.

A shadow came to life behind Bolan, growling, and he saw the wan glow of a distant streetlight glimmer on a gun barrel. Turning to face the threat, thinking he might already be too late, Bolan recoiled from the popping of a handgun rapid-firing from his left.

The shadow stalker crumpled, squeezing off a shotgun blast as he went down. The buckshot scored a rattling hit somewhere across the street, on one of the moored riverboats.

"That's twice I've saved you," the lady said, as she joined him.
"And I still don't know your name," Bolan replied.
"It's Colleen Beacher," she informed him. "With SO15."

5

She saved the rest until they'd cleared the riverfront, putting the killing ground a mile or so behind them. By that time, she had Bolan's name—or, rather, "Cooper's"—but hadn't pried into the purpose of his Glasgow visit.

Yet.

"SO15 is counterterrorism," he observed. "But you were watching Frankie Boyle."

"Or just out for an evening's drive," she said, half-smiling.

"Right. A good Samaritan."

"Maybe my job's arresting Yanks who show up out of nowhere and start murdering Glaswegians."

"Am I under arrest?" he asked.

"Not yet," she said.

"Okay. Strike two."

"You're not a gangster from the States," she said. "I'd smell it on you. So, you're government. Is there a point in asking which department?"

"No. Not really," Bolan said.

"Which leaves us with a bit of a dilemma," Beacher said.

"I'd say you're right," Bolan replied.

"Officially, to keep from getting sacked, I ought to run you in. Of course, you're armed and clearly dangerous, which means we'd likely have to shoot it out and spoil my Ka's upholstery."

The little car had managed to come through their chase and firefight without damage, something of a minor miracle.

"That won't be necessary," Bolan said. "I don't shoot cops."

"No matter what?"

"That's right."

"A man of principle?"

"Something like that." He didn't take the bait or make a joke of it.

"All right. Let's talk, while I decide what happens next. I'm guessing you went after Frankie Boyle for the same reason I've been watching him."

"And that would be…?"

Beacher was hesitant, but after driving two more blocks she took a chance. "Weapons," she said. "He deals in anything that sticks, shoots, or explodes. Some of his customers are on my watch list."

Bolan took his own chance, then. "The TIF, for instance?" he inquired.

"So that's it. Yankee Doodle can't sit still, since Mr. Lockhart bit the dust."

"Call it a motivator," Bolan said. "Nobody wins when mobsters make a profit arming terrorists."

"Is Boyle the end of it for you?"

Bolan studied Beacher's profile, flushed a rosy crimson by the dashboard lights. Another gamble, and he took it.

"I intend to follow where the guns and money lead," he said.

"And keep on killing folk along the way?"

"Not random folk," he said. "The guilty. Unless someone locks them up before I find them."

"We have courts of law in the United Kingdom, Mr. Cooper," she answered stiffly.

"We have plenty in the States, too," he replied. "So, how's that working out for you?"

"I haven't given up on it," she said.

"Me, neither. But I recognize that there are special circumstances that require some special handling."

"Murder," she replied.

"I'd call it surgical excision. Thinning out the predators."

"You're taking quite a risk, telling me this," she said.

He shrugged. "You've seen enough already to convict me. Are you going to arrest me now?"

"Still thinking," Beacher said.

"The good news is that all you've done so far, tonight, is act in self-defense and save my life from one of Boyle's hit-men. Put on the cuffs, now, and you'll likely have a commendation by the weekend."

"Not yet. I'm thinking I should take you to a safehouse first and try to sort this out. I may need some advice."

He frowned at that. "I really can't—"

"From my superiors."

"My crystal ball says they won't sanction us collaborating, if that's what you have in mind."

"I still need the advice. With all that's going on…"

She let that go and drove a while in silence, leaving Bolan to his thoughts. It felt bizarre, him arguing against cooperation with the agent who had saved his life, but she had seen too much to simply let him go and walk away. Conversely, if she took a seat in Bolan's game, she had to go all-in, or it would simply get her killed.

And Bolan had enough ghosts on his conscience, as it was.

"You want to play it safe," he said, "the smart thing is to take me in, then ask for the advice you need."

"Parade you through the station? Set the tongues wagging from Glasgow down to Scotland Yard? I think not."

"Suit yourself," Bolan replied. "This could be a career killer. You could wind up in jail, or worse."

"The safehouse is a mile or so from here," she said, as if he hadn't spoken.

Bolan thought about it. He didn't buy the notion that Beacher had saved him from Boyle's crew to take him somewhere else and put a bullet in his head.

"The safehouse sounds okay," he said. "But if you aren't

arresting me, I've got a car back there with luggage and some things I'd rather not donate to the police."

"Jaysus." She thought about it for another quarter mile, then asked, "You'll follow me, if we go back? We still have things to talk about."

He nodded in the dark and said, "Why not?"

"My CLIENT OBVIOUSLY can't identify the madman who invaded his home and brutally attacked the members of his staff. They'd never met before," Gordon Forbes said.

"It's not so obvious to me," the policeman who had introduced himself as Chief Inspector Malcolm Mair replied. "He's in the line of trade where these things happen, right? A cost of doing business, as we say."

"My client, Chief Inspector, is a well-respected businessman," Forbes said. "If you rely on rumors or refer to ancient history, you'll find yourself misled."

"Did you say ancient history?" Mair challenged. "It was just last week we pulled one Angelo Miscallef from the Clyde—or, rather, what was left of him. This *businessman*'s been fighting the Maltese since last year. He's not forgetting what they did to Ralphie Mungo and his cousin."

"We reject that innuendo categorically, and—"

"Damn the two of you," Boyle injected. "You see me sittin' here?"

The chief inspector smiled, reminding Boyle of a shark. "I absolutely see you, Mr. Boyle. If you'd prefer to speak yourself, instead of through your barrister…"

"I won't allow that," Forbes replied.

"You won't allow?" Boyle pinned Forbes with a glare that silenced him, then turned back to the chief inspector. "You're from the CID, I take it?"

"As you say," Mair granted.

"And I've dealt with you before," Boyle said. "I tell you this—I didn't see who was shootin' up me place, 'cause I was busy with a woman when it started, and I kept me head down after."

"Right. Let's talk about your own boys for a moment, shall we?" Mair replied.

"And what about 'em?"

"Well, you had a lot of company for someone who was… entertaining a young lady, didn't you? And all of them were armed, at that."

"My client is a wealthy man," Forbes interjected, "and a man of influence. We don't deny that certain people would be pleased to see him harmed."

"I didn't ask—"

The barrister pressed on, saying, "The men you are referring to are lawfully employed with Gael Executive Security Consultants and are registered with your department, Chief Inspector."

"Aye, they are," Mair said. "I've seen some of their registrations—and their records. There's Puggy Connolly, for instance. Two years for assault. Doon Hemphill is another. I believe they call him Axman, in the Gorbals."

"'Cause his granddad was a logger," Boyle suggested.

"That explains it," Mair replied sarcastically. "And Ian Garden, also known as Trigger. I suppose he was a big-game hunter in another life?"

"I don't know 'bout that psychic shite," Boyle said, smiling.

"I'm curious to know how some of these *security consultants* cleared their licensing review," Mair said, "considering their charge sheets."

"You should ask the magistrates who certified them, Chief Inspector," Forbes said. "Gael Executive Security submits a list of applicants and trusts in the authorities to do their part."

"And your client holds an interest in this firm, I understand."

"He's an investor, yes," Forbes said.

"In fact, it's a controlling interest, yes?"

"One of his various legitimate concerns. An open book to your department."

"And the more I read, the more it seems a horror story."

"Chief Inspector—"

"Now, you say the firearms found at Mr. Boyle's home have been duly registered and licensed."

"As I'm sure your records will confirm," Forbes said.

"But there's the matter of an illegal machine pistol—a TEC-9, as it's called—found on the outer grounds by one of the responding officers."

"Dropped by the prowler, I assume, as he was fleeing from the scene," Forbes said.

"Well, isn't that convenient?" Mair replied.

"Not for me fellas who was drilled with it," Boyle said. "You seem to be forgettin' who's the victim here, and all."

"I'm not forgetting any of the victims, Mr. Boyle. Nor will I, as we take a closer look at what's behind this morning's mayhem."

"I'm pleased to know you're on the job. Now, if we're done with all this shite…?"

"There's no doubt we'll need to speak with you again," Mair said. "I trust you'll make yourself available at need?"

"Who's need?" Boyle asked.

"To serve the ends of justice, for your friends."

"Of course," Boyle said. "I'm always glad to help the authorities, ain't I?"

"In which case, you're at liberty to go. For now."

"It's been a pleasure, Constable," Boyle said, rising. "Let's do it all again, sometime."

BOLAN FOLLOWED Beacher's Ka back across Glasgow, keeping a bit of distance just in case. At last she nosed her Ford into a carport off an alleyway, got out and waved his Camry up into the space beside her. Bolan grabbed his bags, and moments later they were both inside a two-story row house.

"We're in Langside," Beacher explained. "South of the

Clyde. It wasn't far from here that Mary, Queen of Scots, fought her last battle with Elizabeth the First."

"A lot of history," Bolan said.

"Lots of blood," Beacher replied.

"Same thing," he said.

She nodded, said, "If you're hungry, we keep food here."

"I could eat," Bolan admitted.

"I'm not your cook and bottle washer, though," she said.

"I know my way around a stove," Bolan assured her, wondering if it would be his last meal in the free world. Or his very last, in fact.

"I need a shower," Beacher said. "Go on and make yourself at home."

He found eggs in the fridge and scrambled them in butter, toasted half a dozen slices of white bread, and had it all plated when Beacher came back from her shower. She was in the same clothes, hair a darker red from being wet, and she appeared to be refreshed.

"Smells good."

She sat down at the kitchen table. Bolan set a plate in front of her and said, "There's coffee brewing."

"I could use some."

As they dug into the eggs, he said, "I dropped the ball tonight."

"Oh, yeah? You had some plan in mind besides kicking a hornet's nest?"

Accepting the critique, he said, "I gave some thought to squeezing Boyle for his connection to the TIF."

"And then, what? Travel up the food chain?"

"Pretty much."

"Without the tiresome rules of evidence, indictments and the like."

Bolan met her level gaze, feeling no need to justify himself. "You make that call while you were in the shower?" he inquired.

"Which call?"

"To your superiors."

"Still thinking on it," she replied. "Meanwhile, I've got a story for you."

"I'm all ears," Bolan said.

"Once upon a time, there was a wealthy Highlander who styled himself a laird—that's lord, to you—of all that he surveyed. His family had money, land and influence, a kind of fiefdom as it were. Over the years, the march of progress ate away some of the feudal power and the empire started looking down-at-the-heels. Some say the laird became unhinged. Maybe he schemed and dreamed of ways to bring the old days back again. And he found a gang of young bucks he could use to make it happen."

"Someone propping up the TIF," Bolan said.

"Keeping it afloat with cash as needed," Beacher said. "Most likely pissing in their ears about another war of Scottish independence from the Crown, as if the country has a chance to stand alone. We're twinned with England, for God's sake. Not Siamese, now…what's the proper word?"

"Conjoined?"

"That's it. To get the kind of independence they demand, the TIF would have to sever Scotland from the rest and have it drift away."

"Which brings us to your laird," Bolan said.

"Not *my* laird," Beacher replied. "But he exists, all right. And so far, he's untouchable."

"You want to talk about him? Hypothetically, of course."

She sipped her coffee, nodded and began.

"He's Alastair Macauley, last in line of a clan that fought with William Wallace against Edward Longshanks at Stirling Bridge and Falkirk, then with Edward Bruce at Bannockburn. The movie that you may have seen compressed all that into a year or so, instead of seventeen."

"I missed it," Bolan said.

"No matter," Beacher said. "That's Hollywood, not history. You wouldn't know there was a second war for Scottish independence, if you trust the film. That one dragged on from 1332 to 1357, if you please, with our Macauley's people in the thick of it. And, as you may have noticed, it left Scotland bound to England, no king of their own."

"You think Macauley wants a rematch?" Bolan asked.

"I think he's daft, but rich enough to make some hopeful idiots think that he can pull it off."

"And break up the United Kingdom?"

Beacher shrugged. "When you think about it, how united is the British Commonwealth, these days? The queen's in charge, but only as a figurehead, at least outside of England. How much weight do you suppose she really carries in Australia, Canada, South Africa, or India?"

Bolan wasn't well versed in Scottish politics and didn't want to be sidetracked. Instead of going down that road, he asked, "So, you think this Macauley has a chance?"

"To put himself in charge of independent Scotland?" Beacher answered. "Not a hope in hell. But while he's trying, he and his goons can do untold damage."

"You said he's the last of his line?"

"There was a son, Jerome. He drowned when he was just a teenager. A swimming accident. The laird's a widower. The last Macauley."

"Age?"

"A strapping sixty. Perfect health, by all accounts. He'll be around a while, yet."

"Maybe not," Bolan replied.

"Maybe it's time I made that call," Beacher suggested.

"Waking up the boss at this hour?"

"Or, I could call him from the road tomorrow, I suppose."

"The road?" Bolan leaned backward from his empty plate and asked her, "Are we going somewhere?"

"Did you think a laird would come to us?"

"Where would we find him?"

"At his manor," she replied. "Beside Loch Ness."

Loch Ness, Scottish Highlands: 5:03 a.m.

RONALD MACTAGGART DIDN'T have to check his watch to know that he was running out of darkness. In an hour, more or less, the sun would rise over the Great Glen, burning off the mist. He had to be ashore and well away by then, before the water bailiff spotted him.

Prime poaching hours ran from midnight until four o'clock or so in the morning, but MacTaggart had enjoyed a luck streak this night. His catch included four sea trout, two Arctic char and one Atlantic salmon, which he'd sell to Bryce's shop in Foyers for a weekend's drinking money. Skip a night or two, then come back out and start again.

The lights of Inverfarigaig seemed almost close enough to touch from where MacTaggart sat in his small boat, three hundred yards out from the eastern shore. He gave his baited line a tug, hoping for one more bite before he called it quits, and thought about the dark water beneath his keel.

Loch Ness was Britain's greatest lake. Loch Lomond had a larger surface area, but Ness was vastly deeper, with a maximum confirmed depth of 738 feet off Urquhart Castle, to the west. Some publications cited depths of 820 and 970 feet, but any way you measured it, Loch Ness contained more water than all lakes in England and Wales combined. It was deep enough to sink London's BT Tower with at least 118 feet to spare, or you could sink the London Eye and have 295 spare feet of loch to swim around in, free and clear.

Someone had told MacTaggart that Loch Ness could swallow every man, woman and child on Earth three times over, before it filled up. He didn't know if that was literally true, and didn't rightly care, unless the murky waters tried to swallow him.

And then, there was the monster.

All his life, MacTaggart had heard stories of the water horse or kelpie dwelling in Loch Ness. The tales went back some fifteen hundred years, to Saint Columba's time, when Erin's greatest missionary crossed the Irish Sea to proselytize the heathen Picts. According to Columba's legend, he was traveling along the River Ness when he met locals burying a victim of the kelpie who'd been killed while swimming. Furious, but still a cautious man, Columba used one of his followers to bait the monster, then commanded it to flee. Columba's drenched disciple came ashore intact, but how effective could the ban have been, MacTaggart wondered, when the water beast kept showing up in Loch Ness to the present day?

He sipped a shot of consolation from his flask, then started reeling in his line. The night's catch was better than average, and any morning that he went home safe and dry ranked as a victory.

Make no mistake about it, there was danger on Loch Ness. The water's average temperature was forty-two degrees Fahrenheit, which kept the loch from freezing up in winter, but was cold enough to bring on hypothermia in swimmers—or a fisherman who fell out of his boat. Cold enough to give Loch Ness its reputation as a body of water that rarely surrendered its dead.

Rain squalls were common on the loch, with a record seventy-five inches per year at Fort William and forty-two inches per year at Fort Augustus. Floating logs were hazardous in daylight, doubly so at night. And there were waves that rose without apparent cause to jostle smaller boats, strong enough to tip a passenger—and more likely to dunk one who was tipsy, to begin with.

Race driver John Cobb had died on the loch in 1952, while trying to set a new water speed record in his jet-powered *Crusader,* caught on film as the boat struck something at 206 miles per hour, bounced twice like a skipping stone and then disintegrated. A monument to Cobb stood on the western shore, near Achnahannet—and some folk still believed that the *Crusader* ran afoul of Nessie.

MacTaggart had an outboard motor on his small craft, but he used the oars instead to pull his way shoreward. There was no point in making any extra noise in case the water bailiff might be up early, or working late. Using the lights of Inverfarigaig to guide him, veering slightly to the south, MacTaggart reckoned he would be ashore and on his way before the first pale light of dawn exposed him to suspicious scrutiny.

But what was that? A burbling sound behind him made MacTaggart ship his oars and listen, then turn on his padded seat to scan the water's surface. Not that he could see much, with a bank of clouds obscuring the quarter moon. It might have been a fish, or gas erupting from a mat of rotting vegetation somewhere far below.

Except that, there it was again.

So, what the hell?

MacTaggart's only weapon was the boning knife he carried in his tackle box—and what good would it do against a burping lake? He turned back to his oars and put his back into the rowing, pulled for half a dozen strokes before some large and heavy object struck the hull and nearly jarred him from his seat.

A jolt of panic chilled MacTaggart worse than any night wind off the loch. Dropping the oars, he clutched the small boat's gunwales, hanging on as if sheer force of will could stabilize the rocking craft. Too late, MacTaggart realized that he was going over, and his startled cry deprived him of the chance to draw a final breath before he plunged headfirst into the dark maw of the loch.

6

Bolan and Colleen Beacher spent what was left of the night at the government safehouse. She offered Bolan the second bedroom, but he slept on the living room couch with an angle of fire on both doors, in case someone dropped in overnight.

No one did.

Bolan allowed himself three hours' sleep and woke, from long experience, without resorting to an alarm clock. He was showered and preparing breakfast—eggs again, but fried this time with bacon—by 6:15 a.m. when Beacher emerged from her bedroom, ready to roll.

It went against the grain for Bolan to leave Glasgow without taking care of Frankie Boyle, but he'd agreed with Beacher that the mobster could wait. He sold arms to the TIF and was involved in countless other dirty businesses, but Bolan had a sense that Boyle wasn't going anywhere. Glasgow was that malignant toad's home pond, and if he strayed too far beyond it, other predators might eat him up with tea and scones.

Or was it haggis?

They left Glasgow in Bolan's Camry, following the A82 through various towns to Loch Lomond. It was scenic all the way from there, with vast blue water on their right for miles, but Bolan didn't see a lot of it, forced as he was to focus on the narrow, winding, two-lane road. Blind curves appeared to be the rule, leaving him sandwiched between oncoming traffic and ancient stone walls.

"Is this the high road or the low road?" he inquired after a tour bus swept past them, shivering the Camry in its wake.

"It's neither high nor low, unless you think about our purpose," Beacher said. "For where we're going, it's the *only* road. Be thankful that we have two lanes and lay-bys every hundred yards. If we were heading out to Mallaig, now, you'd see a *narrow* road."

"I'll pass on that, then," Bolan said. But he was already beginning to relax behind the wheel, getting the feel of it. "You make that call yet?"

"Still rehearsing it," she said.

"Well, if you plan to change your mind, you need to do it soon."

"My problem," she informed him. "Did I mention that Macauley's got an expedition up to hunt for Nessie?"

"What? The Loch Ness monster?"

"Aye," she answered, putting on a Highlands accent. "That would be the very same."

"So, he *is* crazy."

"Like a fox, maybe."

"Come on. The monster is a hoax," Bolan replied.

"Don't swallow everything you read without a grain of salt," Beacher suggested. "Years ago, an old man claimed he'd hoaxed one famous picture of the creature. Two reporters held the story back until he died, so nobody could cross-examine him, and even so the story had some gaping holes."

"You think the monster's real?" Bolan asked.

"All I'm saying is, the famous hoax you've read about turned out to be a hoax itself. As for the beastie…well, you know? They've got two exhibitions side-by-side, at Drumnadrochit on the loch. One says the creature's real, the other claims it's not. Both have their share of so-called evidence."

"Okay," Bolan allowed. "But what's Macauley's interest, if

he's not a total flake? How does the monster's legend serve his
war for Scottish independence?"

"Wish I could answer that," she said. "All I can tell you
is that he's financed an expedition with a research boat, new
scanning gear and all, to sweep the loch for evidence."

"Of living dinosaurs?"

"Of something," Beacher said. "It needs a closer look."

They cleared Ardlui, at the far-northern tip of Loch
Lomond, and stayed on the A82 bearing north toward Cri-
anlarich, billed as the Gateway to the Highlands. From there,
Bolan knew, their path continued northward on the fringe of
Rannoch Moor, Glencoe, said to be the "Glen of Weeping" for
a massacre one clan had perpetrated on another there, more
than three hundred years earlier.

More history. More blood.

They passed more lochs along the way, each dark expanse
of water making Bolan think of serpents rising from the
depths, that vision giving way to images of settlers huddled
over fires, in thatch-roofed huts, plotting intrigues against
their neighbors when they weren't at war with Longshanks
and his soldiers.

And it would seem that in present day, a madman had in-
voked those memories to spill more blood on Scottish soil.
And why?

Bolan looked forward to an explanation from the horse's
mouth.

BREAKFAST AT MACAULEY Manor had been prepared in buffet
style, laid out in the grand dining room. The offerings included poached eggs, bacon, link sausage, black pudding,
fried bread, grilled mushrooms and tomatoes, beans and por-
ridge. All the basics to begin a day.

It was a lot of food for just four men, but three of them had
heaping plates when they sat down in high-backed chairs at
one end of a table built for twenty diners. The fourth man, a

withered gnome in a motorized wheelchair, took more modest portions, passing on the pork.

Their host, Alastair Macauley, was a burly man in his mid-sixties, barrel-chested, with a round head planted on a thick neck over broad shoulders. He was dressed in classic tweed, his shock of white hair—only recently receding slightly at the temples—was at odds with his iron-ray mustache and shaggy brows. His ruddy face wore an expression trapped somewhere between a question and a frown.

When all of them were settled, knives and forks in hand, the laird addressed his three companions from the table's head. Bypassing the charade of grace, he growled, "Has any of you heard the news from Glasgow overnight?"

"You mean regarding Boyle?"

The question came from Fergus Gibson, cofounder and commander of the Tartan Independence Front.

"Who else?" Macauley countered.

"He came through all right," Gibson replied. "You can relax about him spilling his guts. It'll never happen."

"He's no concern of mine," Macauley said, "considering that he's your man. If he hangs anyone, it won't be me."

"I'm telling you, it's fine," Gibson said.

"In my dictionary, Mr. Gibson, 'fine' means excellent, superior, worthy of admiration, free of all impurities. Is that how you'd describe your Mr. Boyle this morning?"

Gibson flushed, began to answer, but Macauley cut him off.

"'Fine' can also mean *finished*," the laird informed Gibson. "Completed. At an end. I trust that is the definition that you had in mind?"

Before Gibson could answer, Graham Wallace said, "We have a deal with Boyle, Mr. Macauley."

"*Laird* Macauley," their host said. "And I was not addressing you."

"He's got a point," Gibson said, backing up his second in command. "I can't just tell the man that we aren't doing business with him any more."

"Why tell him anything?" Macauley asked. "He'll get the point when he receives no further orders, eh? And in the meanwhile, he should have his hands full with police, explaining why his men are all shot full of holes."

"Not all of them," Gibson replied. "He has enough left to make trouble for us, if he feels like it."

"In which case," Macauley said, "it is your responsibility to deal with him. I won't have all my plans disrupted by the tantrums of a common criminal."

"We still need weapons," Gibson said.

"Try one of his competitors in that case. If you can't find anyone in Glasgow, then move on to Edinburgh—or London, if it comes to that. I trust we understand each other?"

Gibson nodded, poking at his eggs. "We do."

The stunted figure in the wheelchair made a noise that might have been a smothered giggle or a wheezing breath. At Gibson's elbow, Wallace cleared his throat and said, "We had another glitch last night."

Macauley raised eyes from his meal, fixed Wallace with a baleful glare. "Out on the loch, you mean?"

"'Fraid so," Wallace replied.

"Explain," the laird commanded.

As he listened, hot food cooling on his breakfast plate before him, Macauley felt his anger mounting. He was tempted to lash out at Wallace with his silverware, open his face and get some real blood pudding on the table. When he heard the old man in the wheelchair laughing, it was nearly the last straw.

"Would you explain what's so goddamned amusing, Jurgen?" he demanded.

"These two," the gnomish figure said, pointing the arthritic claw of his right hand across the table toward Gibson and Wallace. "They're like a clown act in the *kabarett*."

"Clowns, are we? If you weren't so feckin' senile, we'd have had it up by now, and—"

"Silence! That's enough!" Macauley roared. "I'll have no

more goddamned mistakes, mishaps, or misadventures. The
next man here who fails me will regret it for the last ten seconds of his life. I hope that's crystal-clear to one and all."

He looked around the table, getting nods from both the TIF
men and a crooked smile from Jurgen. Satisfied, and doggedly
determined not to waste good food, Laird Alastair Macauley
turned back to his plate.

GLENCOE WAS a tourist magnet, drawing hikers, rock climb-
ers and skiers in season, with legions of common sightseers.
Long-distance hikers came on foot, crossing Rannoch Moor
on the same West Highland Way used by British Field Marshal
George Wade to chase Jacobite rebels during the mid-eigh-
teenth century. Motorists bound for the north had no choice
but to pass through Glencoe, and hundreds per day stopped to
browse at its visitors' center.

Clearing the pass, Bolan was greeted by a piper in full re-
galia, performing at a scenic turnout, a West Highland White
Terrier sitting beside him. The haunting strains of "Amazing
Grace" followed Bolan as he drove on past the crowded parking lot.

"What was the trouble here again?" he asked Beacher.

"A feud between the Clan MacDonald and the lowland
Campbells. The MacDonalds were Jacobites, loyal to King
James the Seventh of Scotland, formerly James the Second of
England until he was deposed in 1688. The Campbells sup-
ported William of Orange, which prompted the Maclains of
Glencoe—a branch of the MacDonalds—to raid Campbell
land for livestock. William offered the Highlanders a pardon
in 1691, and the Maclains accepted amnesty."

"So far, so good," Bolan said.

"But the English apparently had their fingers crossed. In
February 1692, they sent the Earl of Argyll's Regiment to
slaughter the Maclain's while they were sleeping. Thirty-eight
men were killed overnight. Forty women and children were

left to die in the snow after their homes were burned. The Highlanders never forget."

"I wouldn't, either," Bolan said.

A sign for the Glencoe Visitors' Centre showed up on his left. At sight of it, Beacher said, "Let's pull in there. I'll make my call while you soak up some history."

"Sounds good," he said, and made the left-hand turn.

A two-lane driveway looped around to Bolan's right and took him past a parking lot reserved for buses and campers— "coaches" and "caravans," as they were known locally—to reach a smaller car park near the buildings. Beacher left the car without another word and headed toward a scenic over-look nearby, while Bolan bypassed the gift shop to enter a long room filled with dioramas and posters depicting Glencoe's creation through upheavals in the prehistoric landscape.

Beacher found him three-quarters of an hour later. There was more pink color in her cheeks than present weather could account for, and her full lips had compressed into a narrow line.

"Ready to go?" she asked him.

"When you are," he answered.

"Right, then."

In the car, he asked her, "So, you're headed back to Glasgow?"

"No," she said. "Rather amazingly, I've got the go-ahead to work with you, prefaced by observations that I must be certifiable to make a move without reporting in beforehand. Once the ranting ended, and my boss had words with someone down in London—who, I'm fairly sure, rang up that number in the States you supplied me with—we've been cleared to proceed."

Bolan frowned and asked her, "Just like that? No argument? No leash?"

"They're trusting in my personal discretion," she replied, voice etched with acid. "And if that sounds like a subtle way of saying my career's stuffed…well, I couldn't argue with you."

"I can take you back," he said. "Or put you on a bus from here."

"A coach."

"Whatever. You can bag it, do your penance and still keep your pension."

They had reached the exit from the parking lot to the A82. A right turn would begin the journey back to Glasgow, while a left would take them on into the Highlands, toward Loch Ness.

"What are you waiting for?" she asked. "Let's go and meet the laird."

"I DON'T BELIEVE I'm hearin' this," Frankie Boyle said. His fingertips were numb from squeezing the cell phone. His temples felt as if an imp in hobnailed boots was kicking at the inside of his skull.

"Sorry as I can be," the caller said, secure in distance from the epicenter of Boyle's wrath. "I'd keep on going, if the choice was mine."

"Whose is it, then?" Boyle demanded.

"My sponsor," Gibson told him. "Says there's too much heat in Glasgow at the moment, and we can't be tied to any of it."

"Heat?" Boyle felt the angry color in his cheeks. "You figure *this* is heat? And what about the stunt your lot pulled with the Yank and all? Didn't that count as heat?"

"That was an action for the cause," Gibson replied. "You understand the difference, I'm sure."

"Oh, aye. When you put heat on me, it's for the holy cause. When strife's comin' at me because of you, it's my fault."

"What do you mean, because of me?"

"You doesn't think this blew up out of nowheres, do you? I've got nothing in works to bring it on myself."

The caller's tone turned sharp. "Was something said? Some kind of message left? What aren't you telling me?"

Boyle felt a wicked smile tugging at the corners of his

mouth. "I'm not tellin' you shite," he said, "since we ain't doin' business anymore."

Boyle cut the link, turned off his cell phone and tucked the device into his pocket. Let the bastard chew on that and see how much he liked the taste, he thought.

It was a petty victory, but Boyle would take what he could get for the time being. While Gibson stewed in his own juice, Boyle had to earn a living with the police on his tail and still find out who'd barged into his home with guns blazing.

It was the kind of insult that demanded a response.

There'd been a bit of bluff behind him blaming Gibson and his Tartan Independence Front for the attack, but just a bit. In fact, he couldn't think of anyone who'd dare to risk that kind of move, no matter what the cops suspected of his usual competitors.

Maltese? Not bloody likely, with their hash and knives.

Not Basil Dunlop's crew, Boyle could say for damned sure, since the best of them were planted in a landfill off St. George's Road.

Hew Alexander? Only if he'd grown new balls since the originals got banjoed in the alley back of Knickers, over Christmas, Boyle thought.

The truth as he believed it was that no other poxy prick in Glasgow—or in all of Lanarkshire, for that matter—had both the nerve and strength to challenge him, Frankie Boyle. Particularly not within the walls of his own home.

Which meant the shite storm was propelled by rage at someone he was doing business with, and Boyle could think of no one but the TIF to blame. He had no beef with the suppliers of his drugs or weapons. All his smuggling routes were clear—or had been, anyhow, until the previous night.

It had to run back to Gibson's gadflies, somehow. Or the sponsor who had just turned off the money tap.

And who was that? Boyle didn't have a clue.

But he was damn sure going to find out.

THE A82 RAN ALONG Loch Leven's southern shore from Glencoe into Lettermore, then crossed a suspension bridge to follow the eastern bank of Loch Linnhe to Fort William. The town had had a surprising seaside look about it, with no end of hotels and B&Bs facing the water.

"It looks like the ocean," Bolan said.

"It is, in a way," Beacher said. "It's a sea loch, fed through Loch Eil by the River Lochy."

"Lochs galore," Bolan said. "Was somebody having a sale?"

She laughed at that, then answered, "What about your Minnesota? Isn't that the Land of Ten Thousand Lakes?"

"You may be right," he said. "I thought it was the Gopher State."

"I'm thinking we should stop for lunch at Spean Bridge," Beacher said, "before we go on up the Glen."

"Suits me."

The last road sign he'd seen put Spean Bridge ten miles farther north. Say fifteen minutes at his present speed, if they avoided getting stuck behind a tour bus or a truck piled with who knew what.

In fact, he shaved five minutes off that estimate. Just before half-past noon they entered the village that had hosted U.S. Army Rangers for assorted training exercises during World War II. They passed the impressive Commando Memorial, depicting three soldiers in bronze and full battle gear, perched on stone with the message "United We Conquer."

Beyond it, the road wound through town until Beacher pointed to a driveway on the right and said, "In here." A sign told Bolan they were entering the Spean Bridge Woollen Mill, but there was no mill to be seen. Instead, he parked behind a good-sized shop and restaurant with covered walkways to its public restroom in case of rain.

The restaurant was cafeteria-style, with a fair choice of sandwiches, salads and hot entrées offered. Bolan ordered Scotch pie and a bowl of soup, not knowing when they'd eat again, while Beacher chose a sandwich and a piece of cake. They found a corner table by the window, no one else within earshot so far, and settled down to eat.

"I've booked a room outside Fort Augustus," she informed him. "There's a loch view and it's close to everything. We're down as man and wife, but don't get any notions."

"Notions aren't my specialty," Bolan replied, and caught her frowning at him with an eyebrow raised, while he tucked into his spicy mutton.

"You realize we can't barge in on Alastair Macauley out of nowhere," she advised him.

"I suppose that would offend a laird," Bolan said.

"Not to mention my superiors," Beacher said. "So far, he's a person of interest, no more and no less. If he turns out to be an innocent eccentric—"

"Then we're wasting time," Bolan said, "when we could be squeezing Frankie Boyle or someone from the TIF for contact information."

"Are all Yanks so impetuous?" she asked.

"I look before I leap," Bolan replied. "But time is always at a premium."

"Just bear in mind we're going north to stop a war, not start one."

"Which assumes the war is already in progress," Bolan said. "The body count corroborates it. And from what I've heard, the TIF is a Degüello kind of outfit."

"Come again?"

"El Degüello," Bolan said. "The Spanish bugle call. No mercy and no prisoners. Santa Anna's army played it at the Alamo, before the final charge."

"John Wayne," she said.

"Among others."

"You're right," Beacher agreed. "They won't negotiate, nor would we offer any terms beyond complete and unconditional surrender."

"Which, I'd say, is—"

"Pretty damned unlikely," Beacher finished for him.

"So, they won't give up their moneyman," Bolan continued. "It's my job to link them up and take them down."

"*Our* job," she said.

"I'm still not sure your people understand the game plan. If they get cold feet after the party's started, there'll be hell to pay."

"I've told you they coordinated with your people in the States."

"All right," Bolan said, "if you trust them not to flip and use you for a scapegoat."

"That's my worry," Beacher told him, picking up her paper plate and wrapper from her sandwich. "Shall we go?"

7

The A82 ran north from Spean Bridge to the eastern shore of Loch Lochy, southernmost in a chain of four lochs that comprised the Caledonian Canal. The third deepest loch in Scotland, it measured nine miles long, but over half of its length lay behind them when Bolan's route met the shore at Letterfinlay. Four miles farther on, they crossed the canal on a swing bridge, shifting to the west bank of another lake.

"Loch Oich," Beacher advised, moments before a road sign validated her announcement. "It's supposed to have its own monster, or did at one time. Locals call the thing Wee Oichy."

"Not a rival for Godzilla, then," Bolan replied.

"I shouldn't think so. Halfway up its length we turn away and cross the River Garry, then swing back to shore. Another swing bridge then, above Loch Oich at Aberchalder, and our next stop will be Fort Augustus, at the south end of Loch Ness."

"And where's that in relation to Macauley's place?"

"His land is on the east side of the loch, near Foyers. He's got something like two hundred acres, with a clear view of the water from his manor."

"Landed gentry," Bolan said.

"With serfs dependent on his generosity," Beacher replied. "Although they're known as laborers these days."

"I'm guessing they won't be involved in his shenanigans with Gibson's gang."

"*Shenanigans* are Irish, but I take your point," she said.

"Macauley isn't fool enough to let his maids and groundsmen sniff around his private business. One we'll have to watch, though, is Ewan MacKinnon, his ghillie."

Bolan frowned at that. "I've heard of ghillie suits," he said, not mentioning that he had worn some, too, on Special Forces missions in another life.

"For sniping, eh?"

"That's right."

"Why am I not surprised? A ghillie is a combination game keeper and hunting guide. On large estates they watch for poachers, deal with predators, preserve the laird's wildlife, then lead him and his guests on shooting walks to kill them."

"And we need to watch MacKinnon why?" Bolan asked.

"Rumor has it that he's equally adept at hunting humans. There've been two trespassers drowned on Macauley's estate in the past five years that I know of. Both ruled accidental, of course, but the forensic evidence was...fuzzy, shall we say?"

"Collusion with a coroner?" Bolan inquired.

"Decomposition and predation," Beacher said. "The folks who vanish on Macauley's land aren't found again until they're ripe and rendered."

"Lovely."

They passed homes, a school and entered Fort Augustus proper from the southwest, with a looming Gothic structure on their right.

"That used to be a Benedictine monastery," Beacher said. "Today it's called the Highland Club, self-catering apartments and cottages. Very upmarket."

"Is that disapproval I hear?" Bolan asked.

She shrugged. "Maybe I'm just a jealous cow. But some things shouldn't change."

The swing bridge at the heart of Fort Augustus was open as they approached. Bolan nosed his Camry up to the barrier and watched the tall masts of a fishing boat creep past, northbound to Loch Ness and, presumably, beyond it into the North Sea. It took a while to pass, and then the bridge swung back around, clearing the traffic lane.

"You're in luck," Beacher said, pointing to their left. "There's Nessie."

Bolan turned and saw a model of a long-necked creature poised beside the roadway, bending as if to feed a smaller version of itself. Both forms were sculpted out of wire, the larger covered in flowers that clung to the mesh.

"Seems harmless to me," Bolan said.

"But you're not in the water," Beacher advised him.

They passed the mooring for a tour boat, shops on their left and a riverside walk to their right. Outside a granite building, people with cameras and flowers cheered for an emerging bride and groom. Then more shops, restaurants, a tourist parking lot—and they were out of town, tracking the loch's long western shore. Beyond the swing bridge stood another, made of stone, spanning the River Oich.

"Our hotel is a half mile ahead," Beacher said. "The Inchnacardoch Lodge. You can't miss it."

She was right again. On Bolan's left, a short half mile from town, a sign proclaimed the Inchnacardoch Country House Hotel. It was a Victorian-era hunting lodge converted to lodgings, all brick with peaked roofs and a vast lawn occupied by several woolly Highland cattle. Bolan turned into the long driveway and followed it around to parking on the hotel's doorstep, elevated sixty feet or so above the loch. Emerging from the car, he had a panoramic view that included a tour boat passing.

No monster anywhere in sight.

Turning, he saw antlers mounted on a whitewashed wall, above the hotel's entrance. He popped the Camry's trunk, retrieved their bags and left the guns, then followed Beacher inside from the parking lot.

THE VESSEL HAD BEEN built in Plymouth. *DeepScan* was fifty-four feet long and had a top cruising speed of eight knots—or ten miles per hour to landlubbers. True to its name, the boat was packed with underwater scanning gear: an ES 60 fish finder and color GPS plotter from Simrad, an Olex 3D seabed scanner, radar with a range of thirty miles and four LCD monitors. In addition to its pilot, it carried a four-man crew.

All five were oath-bound members of the Tartan Independence Front, with Graham Wallace on the bridge, commanding.

"This is a feckin' waste of time," Jimmy Raeburn said, sitting hunched before the bank of monitors, a can of beer in his hand.

People called him "the Cat," because he had a sort of pushed-in nose with freckles on its flattened bridge, and slightly pointed ears. Top off the picture with a mess of red curls that wouldn't yield to any comb, and there was something feral about Raeburn.

"I'll say when it's a waste of time," Wallace replied. "Till then, do as you're told and watch the feckin' screens. Okay, Jimmy?"

"Sure, sure," Raeburn agreed. "I just meant—"

"I know what you meant," Wallace said, interrupting him. "You don't like boats. That's too damn bad."

"Sure, Graham. Not a problem, honestly."

Despite the need for discipline on board the *DeepScan*, Wallace knew what Raeburn and the other crew members were feeling. Whether they were put off by the sailing bit or not, it felt like they were stuck out on the damned loch doing nothing, when they should have been in Glasgow—maybe even down in London—carrying their fight to England.

Wallace, like most other members of the Tartan Independence Front, had only vague ideas of how the world would change should their revolt against the British Crown succeed. There was a list of things he'd memorized—autonomy and liberty, revitalized economy, and so on—but the talking points were vague, with little in the way of evidence to back them up.

So, what? Wallace thought. Did the Americans know how

their country would turn out when they'd risen in arms against crazy old King George the Third? They'd all been flying blind, and you could see how well they'd done by turning on the telly.

Anything was possible.

But miracles, he'd found, occurred most often for the people who prepared themselves, and that took money. Name a poor man who had ever led a major revolution—well, outside of China, anyhow—and Wallace would show you a loser's headstone. No matter what the cause, from charity to civil war, a fat bankroll made all the difference.

"Say, Graham," Henry Bell called, from his starboard window seat. "What happens if we find wee Nessie, after all?"

"We make a million pounds," Raeburn opined.

"Of course we do," Wallace replied. "After we catch it, reel it in alive and find someplace to keep it while the zoos start biddin'. Any one of you sods bring your fishin' tackle?"

No reply to that, and Wallace said, "I didn't think so. Feck the beastie, then. Just keep an eye out for the other, since we know it's down there."

"Do we?" Bell asked him. "Know it's down there?"

Wallace frowned at that. "Macauley says so," he replied.

"Because the old kraut told him," Bell answered back. "How do we know it's not a crock of shite, and all?"

"You want to ask him that, I'll talk to Fergus," Wallace said. "See if he can set up a meeting for you with the laird."

"And that's another thing," Bell pressed on. "Who made him laird of anything? I thought we were about disposin' of the royals and that."

"The *English* royals," Raeburn chimed in, and took another sip of beer.

Wallace killed the debate by shifting gears. "Henry, it's your turn on the monitors," he said. "Jimmy, go up and see if Colin wants more coffee."

Raeburn seemed about to protest, but he instantly thought better of it, rose and moved out toward the wheelhouse. Bell took his place before the screens where colors changed with depth and objects on the bottom were revealed in outline, subject to interpretation by the viewer.

"Hope I know the damn thing if I see it," Bell said.

"Should be no doubt about it," Wallace said. "Two hundred and twenty feet long, it's not easy to miss."

"We've been doin' a fair job so far," Bell replied. "And who says that it's still in one piece?"

"May be better for us if it's not," Wallace said. "Close to eight hundred tons for the lot."

"Jaysus Christ! You expect us to lift that and all?"

"Don't be daft. We'll be usin' the laird's toy for that."

"And which fools get the honor?" Bell asked.

With a smile, Wallace said, "I was thinking of you."

THE INCHNACARDOCH Lodge's lobby, lounge and stairs to Bolan's left were carpeted in a dramatic tartan pattern, red and black predominating. At the registration desk, a smiling hostess welcomed them. The jet-black Labrador retriever at her feet was smiling, too, beating a tattoo on the carpet with his tail.

Bolan signed in, using his Cooper ID and credit card. Their room was number 10, at the far end of the first-floor hall. Newly remodeled, they were told, with a Jacuzzi tub in the ensuite. Dinner was served between seven and nine, with breakfast the same in the morning. They declined help with their bags and made the trek upstairs.

"Looks like the bridal suite," Beacher said, teasing Bolan, as they stepped into a spacious room with a four-poster. "Do you suppose she noticed that we don't have rings?"

"Makes us a modern couple, I suppose," Bolan replied.

Beacher unpacked her bag while Bolan studied Loch Ness from their window. A boat made its slow way along the far shore, one man on deck, at least two vaguely visible through tinted windows.

"Is this Macauley's monster-hunting boat?" he asked.

Beacher was at his elbow in an instant, Bolan shifting to provide her with a view. "I can't make out the name from here," she said. "His is the *DeepScan*. What he's playing at is anybody's guess."

"Something to check on," Bolan said. "I'd like to see his place as soon as possible."

"From land or water?" Beacher asked.

"Let's try the water first," Bolan replied. "We're less obtrusive on a tour boat than cruising past his gate in daylight."

"Anytime you're ready, then," she said.

Their room keys were attached to brass fobs six or seven inches long. Beacher slipped hers into her handbag; Bolan tried a couple of his pockets and decided he would hide it in the Camry when they got downstairs.

The black Lab saw them off and might have trailed them to the Camry if his owner hadn't called him back. Leaving the hotel's driveway, Bolan turned across oncoming traffic and back toward Fort Augustus, for the short run to the tourist parking lot. He found a space close by the information center, scored a free map of the district from a rack inside the open doorway and joined Beacher for the stroll through town, to reach the dock where tour boats berthed and sailed.

The walk took them past shops, row houses and a busy restaurant, across the swing bridge—closed this time, no boats awaiting passage—and beyond the point where they had seen the wedding party. There were more shops and restaurants across the way, before their path would take them to the monastery-cum-hotel. Each shop they passed had monster souvenirs on sale: plush Nessies of all sizes, long-necked glass and plastic dragons, monster key chains and erasers, monster T-shirts, comic postcards.

The tour boat sailed again at three o'clock, which left them time to kill after procuring tickets. They walked along the canal, three hundred yards or so, until they reached a concrete pier protruding like a finger raised to probe Loch Ness. From where they stood, the loch seemed to go on forever, flanked by steep hillsides that plunged below the surface into depths that never saw sunlight.

"There might be anything down there," Beacher observed.

"I guess," Bolan replied. "Smart money says Macauley isn't hunting for an undiscovered species, though."

"It wouldn't help his cause, I grant you," Beacher said. "But I can't suss out what he's up to."

"We may have to ask him," Bolan said.

"Lairds tend to resent intrusion," she replied.

"I feel the same way about terrorism," Bolan said, pausing briefly before going on. "We should have brought binoculars."

"I have a small pair in my bag," Beacher said. "Good enough for checking out the manor when we pass it, anyhow."

A breeze came off the loch and found its way through Bolan's clothing to his skin. Again, he pictured tribes of Highlanders hunched over fires at night, trying to keep the chill and dark at bay.

"It's beautiful," he said at last. "But you can feel the harshness underneath. It gives me a new respect for pioneers."

"Do you know anything about the Highland clearances?" she said.

"Some kind of sale?" he asked.

"Nothing to joke about with locals," Beacher said. "During the eighteenth and the early nineteenth centuries, landlords from England drove the Highland natives from their homes by any means available, replacing them with herds of sheep. A cholera epidemic and a potato famine rivaling Ireland's finished the job, clearing out two thousand families a day at the peak of it. We'll never know how many starved or died from other causes, but three-quarters of the Gaelic-speaking population disappeared."

"Plenty of room for grievance, then," Bolan replied.

"But not Macauley's kind," she said. "His lot were never dispossessed."

Bolan glanced at his watch and said, "We'd better get back to the boat."

"One Scottish monster coming up," Beacher replied, and fell in step beside him.

THEIR TOUR BOAT, the *Royal Scot,* was roughly the same size as Alastair Macauley's *DeepScan,* equipped with similar scanners but fitted with upper-deck seating for sixty passengers and sheltered seats for sixty more below. A well-stocked bar completed the amenities.

Bolan and Beacher were close to the front of the line as they boarded, securing window seats belowdecks near the bow. As they sat, Beacher nudged Bolan in the ribs and told him, "There's your monster."

Glancing to his left, he found a small window decal depicting a miniature long-necked creature in silhouette. Once they had sailed, he understood, a photo snapped from inside the cabin would seem to show Nessie emerging to starboard, some distance away.

"I'm guessing that's the closest that we'll come to one," he said.

"You never know," Beacher replied.

It took ten minutes for the other passengers to board, then their skipper began the delicate process of backing away from the dock. Five minutes later, the *Royal Scot* was motoring north, Fort Augustus receding behind them. A live voice emerging from speakers throughout the interior cabin began to regale them with statistics on the loch's dimensions and anecdotes from its history.

Bolan listened with part of his brain, while he watched the depth monitors mounted above the bow windows. From Fort Augustus onward, the loch grew increasingly deeper, its bed dropping away below them toward record depth logged off Urquhart Castle on the west bank, several miles ahead. Bolan saw nothing on the screens that looked like swimming dinosaurs, but he was no expert at reading high-tech sonar, either.

"Half a mile until we pass Macauley's place," Beacher informed him. As she spoke, she took a pair of Bushnell Elite custom compact binoculars from her purse and held them ready in her lap.

"You must have been a Girl Scout," Bolan said.

"Girl *Guide,* on this side of the water," she corrected him. "But yes, I like to be prepared."

About that time, the captain's voice announced that mountain goats were visible above the *Royal Scot,* to their right. It gave Beacher the perfect opportunity to raise her small field glasses, scanning for their target.

"There," she said, pointing as she handed the binoculars to Bolan. He used one finger to adjust the focus and saw a huge stone structure perched atop the hillside, windows like a row of spider's eyes commanding a panoramic view of the loch. There was a dock and boathouse below, with steep stairs leading upward, with some kind of lift beside them.

"No safe access from this side," he said, keeping his voice low-pitched.

"I wouldn't want to climb that in the dark," Beacher agreed.

Or daylight, either, Bolan thought. One halfway decent rifleman could stop an army coming up the hillside on those stairs, exposed. Give him some cover, and they'd never reach the top.

"Okay," he said, returning the binoculars. "The other side it is, then."

"Look before you leap," the SO15 agent advised. "The property is fenced and guarded."

"Right," Bolan replied. "The ghillie."

"At the very least. For all I know, he might have a small army on the grounds."

Time for reconnaissance.

Some thirty minutes out, the *Royal Scot* turned for home, her skipper directing their attention to specific points of interest on the western shore. Bolan thought normal tourists on the cruise should be well satisfied—particularly those who'd patronized the bar—but he'd learned little that would help him tackle Laird Macauley in his lair.

When they were halfway back to Fort Augustus, Bolan saw a small police boat off their port side, two men in fluorescent chartreuse vests bent over the gunwale, hauling at something in the water. Closer, and he saw it was a human body, tangled in what seemed to be a fishing net.

The *Royal Scot*'s captain tried to redirect his squeamish passengers' attention to the far side of the loch, but Bolan focused on the small drama unfolding as they passed. While it was difficult to say with any certainty, the corpse looked fairly fresh.

Cold water? Or a recent death?

Coincidence, or something else?

"Can you find out what happened here?" he asked Beacher.

"I should be able to," she said. "Likely a simple accident."

"Let's hope so," he replied.

The skipper did his part to liven up the last bit of the tour, but one tourist abovedecks had reacted badly to the water-logged cadaver, and a cabin boy was busy with a mop and pail. Bolan had no idea how many people drowned at Loch Ness during any given year, but reckoned the police should have at least a general idea. They wouldn't share with him, nor was he anxious to approach them, but Beacher could likely badge her way past any rote objections and secure preliminary information on the latest incident.

And Bolan hoped it was coincidence.

If Alastair Macauley was involved with terrorists, he had enough to answer for already.

And the tab was coming due.

8

The police station in Fort Augustus was a two-man operation with a hotline to the Northern Constabulary's headquarters in Inverness. Colleen Beacher knew that she might trigger alarms by barging in and questioning the local constables, but since she had secured the backing of her own superiors in London, she believed the risk to be minimal.

Unless, of course, her wealthy target had a local friend in uniform.

Beacher found the station house on the southwestern outskirts of Fort Augustus. They had passed it coming in, on the A-82, and she had made a mental note of its location from the blue-and-chartreuse sign outside. The officer who greeted her was decked out in the standard uniform: white shirt, black tie, black slacks and shoes. His stab-resistant belt with two-way radio attached at shoulder level bore a stenciled POLICE logo in place of a badge. His duty belt creaked lightly when he moved, and she could see his baton on the desk behind him, beside a checkered cap.

"Yes, ma'am," the young man said. "May I help you?"

Beacher showed her ID and introduced herself. The officer blinked once at mention of SOI5.

"Security Service, is it? We don't see much of you lot in Fort Augustus." With a smile, he added, "None at all, in fact, since I've been here."

"Routine investigation," Beacher said, watching his eyes

dip toward her chest, then bounce back to her face. "I'm curious about a body in the loch."

"Och, aye." The smile vanished. "Likely a fisherman, from what I understand. The water bailiff found a boat adrift, then spied the body. Since it's nothing to do with poaching and the like, he passed it off to us."

"ID?" she asked.

He frowned. "You mean the floater?"

"Right." A test of patience, but she passed.

"Ronald MacTaggart, from the wallet in his pocket. Home address in Foyers. That's along the east side—"

"I know where it is," she cut him off. "Who's handling the FAI?"

There were no coroners in Scotland. Public prosecutors—known as procurators fiscal—convened fatal accident inquiries on any suspicious deaths, generally conducted by a sheriff court equivalent to a justice of the peace in other jurisdictions. The sheriff may employ pathologists as needed to determine cause of death. In the event of homicide, all evidence available was then delivered to an advocate-depute for prosecution before the High Court of Justiciary.

"They'll send him up to Inverness," the constable replied, "and then release him to the family, if any, when they're done with him."

"You didn't know MacTaggart personally?" Beacher asked.

"No, ma'am. If he was prone to poaching, you might ask the water bailiff. Liam Abercrombie, that would be."

"And I would find him...where, again?"

"Right here," he said. "By which, I mean to say in Fort Augustus. Liam shares an office with the local registrar, on Oich Road at the Highland Council service point. Memorial Hall, that would be. It's on the channel by the ferry landing. Hard to miss, ma'am."

Beacher recalled the wedding party. "Just across from where the tour boat docks," she said.

"The very same. There's nothing very far from anything in Fort Augustus."

"Makes it simple," she replied. "Thanks for your help."

"Always a pleasure, ma'am," he said.

"I need to keep this visit confidential," Beacher said. "You'll help me out with that, I trust?"

"Of course! A pleasure, as I say."

And Beacher felt him watching as she left.

It wasn't quite a wasted trip, but if she'd known the water bailiff was her man, she could have saved the hike. As Beacher doubled back toward town, she wondered if Cooper was making any headway on his part of it. He planned to track the *DeepScan,* heading for a shop that rented motorboats to fishermen, and Beacher hoped he wasn't biting off too much, his first day on the scene.

If anything went wrong…

The agent dismissed that thought. Whoever Cooper was representing, whatever his real name might be, he'd survived in the trade so far without her second-guessing his plans. Beacher knew she should be more concerned with herself, her career and survival, instead of a man she had known less than twenty-four hours.

And take out insurance, she thought. If he blows it, make sure there's a way to get clear.

That defeatist train of thought disgusted and embarrassed her, but it was part of day-to-day survival in the bowels of a bureaucracy. No one was simply free to do the job he or she had signed on for, without considering the politics involved and how a split-second decision might rebound to scuttle a career.

Turning off Station Road with open parkland opposite, she moved past gift shops and a restaurant, then crossed before she reached the swing bridge. From the sidewalk she could see a green Land Rover parked outside of Memorial Hall, with an emblem of the Highland Salmon Fishery Board.

Somebody's home, Beacher decided, picking up her pace.

"STILL NOTHIN'," Jimmy Raeburn said, as he heard Graham Wallace coming up behind him. There was no mistaking those boots on the *DeepScan*'s vinyl flooring.

"Never mind," Wallace replied. "We're checkin' every inch."

Because the feckin' laird says so, Raeburn thought but kept it to himself. He'd already said more than was entirely safe about the boring search. If Wallace mentioned his complaint to Gibson or Macauley, nasty repercussions might follow.

Raeburn hailed from East Kilbride, in South Lanarkshire, where he'd grown up poor and bitterly resenting charity from people who were better off. He wasn't one of those who hated England from the cradle up, but natural defiance of authority and falling in with bad companions predisposed him to rebel. That attitude had cost him time in jail on several occasions, and his life was going nowhere in a hurry when he'd met an older fellow who was wrapped up in the Cause.

And here he was, staring at monitors while riding up and down Loch Ness, wishing a monster *would* pop up and give the boat a shaky-waky, just to break up the monotony. It was a funny way to run a revolution, if he did say so himself.

Of course, it was the so-called laird's idea, and Gibson couldn't seem to turn him down. Raeburn knew all about the cash Macauley had invested in the TIF—well, he knew some of it; enough to know the old man was a major benefactor—but you had to draw the line somewhere. Suppose, Raeburn wondered, the old fart gave the TIF a million pounds and said they had to spend it hunting fairies at the bottom of his garden? What would Gibson say, besides, "Yes, sir"?

Twelve hours coming up, since they had started out that morning, and the night work still lay waiting. Raeburn thanked his lucky stars he wasn't part of *that*. Cruising the surface all day long was bad enough, but plummeting into the depths after the sun went down was something else entirely.

And then there was the dead man. No problem, if the powers that be decided it was death by misadventure. Raeburn wasn't sure exactly what a misadventure was, but lately he'd suspected that he might be having one. It sure as hell wasn't the adventure he'd expected when he'd joined the Tartan Independence Front.

They talked a good game, Gibson and his buddy Wallace. And they had delivered, to a point. Raeburn had helped to build some bombs that made a bit of noise on the telly, and the Yank they'd snuffed in Glasgow definitely caused a stir. They had a long way yet to go before they claimed a victory, but getting there was more than half the fun.

When he'd signed on, Raeburn was thinking of the IRA in Belfast, all the action they had seen and the respect that they'd commanded. Fighting on for years and years before Raeburn was born, whole generations of combatants raised to flout the English law and wade in blood to reach their goal.

But riding up and down a lake to look at fish?

Not bloody likely.

He wasn't giving up, mind you. The TIF was still the closest thing to family that Raeburn had discovered since he was expelled from school and his old man had thrown him out for tarnishing the Raeburn name. His kinfolk had been dead to Raeburn since that day, but not forgotten, and whenever he was lifted by the coppers, Raeburn hoped they were embarrassed yet again.

Petty? Hell, yes, he realized. Satisfying, too, at the same time.

Beneath his feet, the rumble of the *DeepScan*'s engine changed. Raeburn could feel the boat begin a wide, slow turn. He wondered if they were about to start another pass along the loch, as if twelve hours was enough to satisfy the bloody laird this day.

His stomach growled, whether from hunger or his last beer he couldn't say. They ate well at Macauley's place, no denying it, but steak and tatties only went so far toward satisfying any warrior dedicated to a holy cause.

Some action would be nice, and Raeburn hoped that he

would see some soon. If nothing else, maybe he could sneak off to Inverness over the coming weekend, find himself a stunner who would take his mind off fishy business at the loch.

"We're headin' back," Wallace called from the companionway. "Keep a sharp lookout on those screens until we're at the dock."

"Aye-aye," Raeburn replied, watching the sonar pick out salmon, trout and char by size, in different colors. All so bloody fascinating, he could barely stay awake.

Fort Augustus: 4:50 p.m.

BOLAN RENTED the boat from the old codger who had three on hand for fishermen. It measured fifteen feet and had a vintage British Seagull outboard motor bolted to its stern. The old man raised an eyebrow when he noted Bolan's lack of any fishing gear, but still took cash enough up front to replace the boat twice over, in case Bolan sent it to the bottom of the loch.

The soldier puttered out from dockside, following the same channel he'd traveled on the *Royal Scot,* earlier. The small boat handled well enough, the motor running loud but smoothly. On his right, the former monastery had a nice medieval look about it from a distance, hard to visualize the modern luxury inside. Its spacious immaculate grounds, looked like a perfect spot for golf and horseback riding, although neither sport was physically in evidence.

Beyond the channel, Bolan held a steady course northward, staying two hundred yards or so out from the eastern shoreline on his right. He'd brought his map, to help with landmarks, such as the stone pyramid commemorating the death of Winifred Hambro, a banker's wife who vanished into Loch Ness when her family's boat capsized in 1932. Beneath that monument lay Corrie's cave, the reputed hideout of an eighteenth-century rebel who tried to assassinate Prince William, Duke of Cumberland, during the Jacobite rebellion.

Blood and history, wherever Bolan turned.

The loch was relatively calm as he motored northward. Only a mile and a half across at its widest point, but at twenty-five miles in length, the loch seemed vast from his seat in the small rented boat. Away to his left, the Inchnacardoch Lodge looked like a hotel from a child's Monopoly game, small enough to cover with the tip of Bolan's thumb.

And what if he should meet a real-life monster on the loch? He wore the big Beretta 93-R in its shoulder rig, but would a handgun help at all, against a prehistoric dragon? Bolan doubted it would, and while he put no stock in legends, cruising on the loch alone, mere inches from the water's surface, left him with a brooding sense that anything could happen.

Soon enough, he reached the point where Alastair Macauley's mansion loomed above the loch, its narrow staircase and electric lift descending steeply to a pontoon dock below. Bolan supposed the lift was used for hoisting cargo brought from Inverness or Drumnadrochit, even up from Fort Augustus if Macauley's people didn't feel like driving two or three miles overland to shop.

As Bolan passed, the lift was running, easing down the hillside with two passengers aboard. He couldn't stop and stare, but Bolan registered that both were men, one standing, while the other sat. A wheelchair, possibly? But why were they descending, with no boat on hand to carry them away?

He got his answer moments later, when he met the *Deep-Scan* coming home. One of its crewmen was on deck, smoking a cigarette, the others merely shadows in the wheelhouse and belowdecks, through the bank of tinted windows. Searching— but for what?

He didn't buy the image of Macauley as an aging crypto-zoologist, trying to prove that Nessie existed. But if the cover story was false, why waste time and bucketsful of cash scanning the loch's abyssal depths? How did it serve the Scottish revolution bankrolled by Macauley—if, in fact, Beacher was right about the laird's involvement with the Tartan Independence Front?

Bolan nodded at the *DeepScan* as he passed, observing standard boater's etiquette, and didn't start his southward turn until he'd traveled for another quarter mile or so along his present course. It wouldn't do to tip the vessel's captain to the fact that he was being tailed, so Bolan swung out farther toward the middle of the loch for his return to Fort Augustus.

The *DeepScan* was already nosing in to dock as Bolan overtook it, churning southward. Casually, he palmed his cell phone, raised it as if checking for a signal—there was none—and peered at the sky as if the answer to his problem hovered there. From that pose, Bolan keyed the video recording function, zoomed it to the max and held the phone as steady as his small craft would allow until he'd passed Macauley's wharf.

Next it was back to Fort Augustus and Beacher, to see what she had learned from the police and try to match the faces he had captured, if they were in focus, to the TIF or any known associates.

BEACHER FOUND Liam Abercrombie in his tiny office at Memorial Hall, filling out what she supposed had to be an accident report. He was a slender man with hair nearly the color of his deeply tanned and weathered face. If Beacher hadn't known he was the water bailiff, she'd have pegged him as a fisherman, perhaps a hunter's guide.

She badged him, introduced herself and shook his callused hand. With evident reluctance, Abercrombie nodded toward the small room's only vacant chair and waited while she sat.

"Before we start," she said, "I need to ask that you hold anything I say in strictest confidence."

"Oh, aye? And why is that?" he asked.

"I'm in the midst of an investigation, and it's classified," Beacher replied.

"Like national security, you mean?"

"Like that, exactly."

"Och," he said, rising a little taller in his swivel chair. "I'd best pay close attention, then. Some kind of Russian spy ship sneaking down through the canal, is it? A plot to make our sheep go bald, and all?"

Frowning, she said, "I'm not James Bond."

"No, ma'am. You surely aren't—although you may know, he was Scottish on his dad's side."

"What I've come to ask about is the MacTaggart drowning," Beacher said.

The water bailiff sighed and shook his head. "Old Ronnie, eh? It figured that the loch would claim him someday, I suppose."

"And why is that?"

"His poaching. Kept himself in drink with that."

She raised an eyebrow and asked, "You were aware of his activities?"

"Of course," Abercrombie said. "I'm the one who lifted him and fined him half a dozen times over the past six, seven years. Reckon I caught him once for every twenty-five or thirty trips he made."

"So, a persistent violator, then."

"Persistent and consistent," Abercrombie said. "Old Ronnie had his steady list of customers, you know. In Foyers, Fort Augustus, up as far as Portclair on occasion. Restaurants and shops could always count on Ronnie for a decent shake."

"And now he's dead."

"Aye, so he is. It happens, eh?"

"How often, would you say?" Beacher inquired.

"To Robbie? Just the once."

Resisting the impulse to snap at him, she said, "Drownings, I mean. Within your bailiwick."

"Not often, hereabouts," he answered. "Ronnie is our first this year, in fact. Had two last year, but both of them fell out of the same boat. I ask you, ma'am, who takes a boat out, if they's never learned to swim?"

"Could Ronnie swim?" she asked.

"Oh, aye. Part eel, I'd guess he was. Swum with the best of them."

"So, then…what happened, do you think?"

"From what I saw, fishin' him out, he'd banged his head," Abercrombie said.

"How would that go?" she inquired.

"The loch can be a right bitch, if you'll pardon me. Look smooth as glass one minute, then a wave comes up from no-where and you're rockin' fit to topple. Some'll tell you it's the beastie. Ronnie could've lurched and hit his head, then fallen overboard. Tried comin' up and beaned himself against the hull."

"You saw head injuries?" she asked.

"I did, ma'am," Abercrombie answered. "Here…and here." He aimed an index finger to his temple first, then drew it around behind his ear.

"Two impacts."

"Could've happened like I said."

Or someone could have bludgeoned him, she thought. But why?

"You said he poached for local restaurants and shops?"

A silent nod across the desk.

"No individuals who dealt with him, at all?" Beacher in-quired.

"I wouldn't be surprised to hear his neighbors got a trout from time to time, an' all. That Ronnie was generous to his friends."

"But would he sell to private individuals?" she pressed.

The water bailiff countered with a question of his own. "Like who?"

She shrugged. "I don't know any locals. You tell me."

He thought about it for a moment, or pretended to, then said, "Can't think of anyone, offhand. Which is to say, I never caught him sellin' private, like. I couldn't rule it out, but I see nothing to do with national security and all in poaching fish."

"I'm sure you're right," she said. "What are your thoughts about the latest monster hunt?"

"Well, now…I won't say nothin's out there, will I? Even

though I've never seen the kelpie for myself, there's many I respect and trust who have. Some tourists, too," he added with a half smile.

"Does it strike you odd that Alastair Macauley would invest so much in searching for the creature after all this time?"

"Who knows? The wealthy aren't like you or me," Abercrombie said. "One of them gets a notion in his head, he's got the time and money to indulge it. For all I know, the laird's been interested in the beastie all his life, but just now took a notion to investigate. Nobody faults him spendin' money where it does some good."

"Have you met any of the people he's got working for him?" Beacher asked.

"Aboard the boat, you mean?"

"That's right."

"I introduced myself, when they first got here," Abercrombie said. "Not locals, but they seem all right. Respectful, like."

Beacher sensed his reserve and didn't push it. She thanked the water bailiff for his time and left, without reminding him to keep his mouth shut. If he planned to betray her out, a second warning wouldn't matter.

And it might identify another enemy.

9

The chairlift was a slow, noisy contraption, gumbling and groaning as it carried Jurgen Dengler in his wheelchair up the steep hillside from Loch Ness to the house above. A breeze rippled his thinning, snow-white hair and made him shiver slightly, even underneath his heavy overcoat.

Dengler rode the lift alone on his return trip to the mansion on the bluff. Gibson had ridden down with him, a point of courtesy, but had chosen to climb the staircase with his crewmen from the *DeepScan,* going back. Two of the small-fry hurried on ahead, likely to slake their thirst for alcohol, while Wallace stayed with Gibson, keeping pace with Dengler's lift. They chattered aimlessly along the way, discussing nothing in particular, while Dengler scanned the loch with cold gray eyes.

Watching a motorboat that passed the doch below, southbound to Fort Augustus, Dengler frowned and said, "I've seen that one before."

Gibson and Wallace turned to see what he was looking at, tracking the small boat on its way. The lone man at the tiller held something before his face, examining it.

"Just a fisherman," Wallace said.

"Nobody," Gibson agreed.

To Gibson, Dengler said, "You didn't notice him, as we were coming down? He passed the other way, northbound."

"I musta missed it," Gibson said, entirely unconcerned.

"Those little boats all look alike," Wallace said.

"One man, with no fishing gear," Dengler observed. "Making a round-trip in such a short time? Where, we may ask, was he going?"

"Now you mention it," Wallace said, "he could be the same fella who passed us on the loch afore."

"Could be? You are not certain?" Dengler challenged.

"No," Wallace replied. "I didn't pay attention to 'im, special. Folk go boatin' on the loch, ya know."

"Certainly," Dengler said. "But do you notice if they follow you, perhaps?"

"Ya think he…? No, he never," Wallace said.

"I would prefer to know, instead of guessing," Dengler said, this time addressing Gibson.

"Aye," Gibson replied. "And me, as well."

Wallace could not conceal the angry flush that tinged his cheeks at that. "Fergus," he said, "you think I'd miss somethin' like that?"

"There's no harm making sure," Gibson replied. "It costs nothing if we send a couple of the boys to ask around in town. Check out the boat-hire spots and all."

Dengler felt Wallace glaring at him and was unconcerned. The Scotsman could not touch him— or would rue it to his dying moment, if he did. Dengler might be old and crippled, but he was not without influence. Unless he'd lost his mind, Wallace would not risk Alastair Macauley's wrath to harm him.

The motorboat had vanished by the time they reached the halfway point between Macauley's private dock and his stone mansion on the summit. Dengler chafed to hear what Wallace and his crew had found today, if anything, but instinct told him to be ready for another disappointment. If they had discovered what they sought, he would have already known. Wallace would certainly have spilled the news to Gibson, or at least hinted around it, in defiance of Macauley's order that he be the first to know.

So, nothing yet.

Dengler was not discouraged, but he knew that every passing day wheeled him a little closer to the grave. Some might say he had lived on borrowed time since 1945, but he finally had the verdict of physicians that his days were numbered. Six months, one had said. Another guessed that he might last a year. The third refused to speculate in finite terms, but urged him to be expeditious in arranging his affairs.

And so he had.

The work at Loch Ness was his last unfinished task. It would not be completed as intended, from the outset, but at least his early efforts might not be entirely wasted. If he succeeded here, Dengler could reach out from beyond the grave to smite his enemies. And they would know exactly who had wounded them, when the communiqué he'd left with his lawyer in Zurich reached *The Times, The Independent* and *The Guardian.* Whatever happened after that was immaterial.

But in the meantime, nothing could disrupt the plan that he had hatched with Macauley. No distractions could prevent the search from going forward to fruition. After decades of delay, he could not fail.

Frustration set his teeth on edge, and Dengler drew a deep breath, holding it to calm himself. Gibson might be a lunatic, deluded in his dream of separating Scotland from the British monarchy, but he was adept at relatively simple tasks—such as planting bombs; eliminating minor cogs from the machinery of empire; squeezing information from a hostage, if it came to that.

He was a tool, but useful in his way.

And there was still time to eliminate a threat, if one existed. On the other hand, if Dengler cast fatal suspicion on a hapless tourist...well, bad luck for him.

The strong survived and subjugated the weak.

So it had always been. So would it always be.

BOLAN MET BEACHER at the tourist car park, handing her his cell phone after they were seated in the Camry. While he drove back to the lodge, she watched the video he'd shot of the *DeepScan,* its crew and the men who had come down to meet it.

"The fellow who's tossing the lines out is James Raeburn, Jimmy 'the Cat' to his friends. That's Fergus Gibson catching, so we've literally tied Macauley to the Tartan Independence Front. And there comes Graham Wallace from belowdecks."

Slowing for the hotel's driveway entrance, Bolan said, "I don't suppose you recognize the old man in the wheelchair."

"Sorry, no," Beacher replied. "There's no one like him on the TIF rosters."

"An educated guess, then?" Bolan prodded, as he slowed around the last curve of the driveway, nosing toward a parking space.

"He's ancient from the look of him," Beacher said. "Even if he's old-guard Tartan Army, he'd have been middle-aged or older when it started in the seventies."

"And since Macauley has no family…"

"That's it. Another mystery," she affirmed.

"Just what we need," Bolan replied, setting the Camry's brake and switching off the engine.

"Send that footage to my cell," Beacher suggested, "and I'll e-mail it to London. Do the same with your crowd, and between us, maybe we'll get lucky with a facial recognition hit."

Resigned to waiting, Bolan pushed the necessary buttons on his cell phone, waited thirty seconds for a minor miracle of cyberspace, then told Beacher, "You've got it."

They found the black Lab waiting for them in the hotel lobby, and were forced to pay a toll by scratching him around the ears. Their hostess came from dusting in the lounge, inquired about their day and asked if they were dining in.

"Indeed we are," Beacher replied. "Seven o'clock, I think you said?"

Bolan confirmed the time with a nod before they made their way to their room.

They had agreed that, since full dark would not descend over the Highlands until half-past eight or later, they should eat at the hotel and set out afterward for a drive-by view of Macauley's estate.

Once in their suite, Bolan opened his map on the four-poster and Beacher traced their route with a finger.

"We go back through town to the point where we entered," she said, "then keep left at the abbey, instead of following the A82. That puts us on the Glendoe Road, named for the lodge, also known as the B862. We loop around the south end of the loch, here, and veer off toward Loch Tarff and beyond. It's sheep country out there, losing sight of Loch Ness, but we don't take it all the way. There's a split beyond Whitebridge, where the B852 branches off and comes back to shore at Foyers."

"Where the poacher lived," Bolan observed.

"The very same. And not far from Macauley's land. From there, the B852 runs north along the eastern shore to Dores, where it joins up with the B862 again. Confused yet?"

"I can handle it," Bolan replied.

"Our greatest danger will be getting spotted on the B852. It's narrow two-lane all the way, with woods and farmland on your right, and a sheer drop into Loch Ness on your left. There'll be no place to turn around between Foyers and Dores, unless we pull into someone's private drive."

"I need the recon," Bolan told her. "If you'd rather sit it out…"

"Did I say anything about me sitting anywhere?" she asked.

"No, but—"

"Don't 'but' me, Cooper. If I want out of this arrangement, you will be the first to know."

"Does this mean that the honeymoon is over?" Bolan asked.

"I told you not to get any ideas," Beacher replied.

"Okay. Unless you want the shower first…?"

"Go on ahead. I'll make some coffee."

"Black for me," he said, "if that's not out of line."

"It isn't in my job description, but I'll let it go this time," she said with the suggestion of a smile.

The shower was a handheld nozzle on a hose that came out of the wall above the large Jacuzzi tub. In other circumstances, Bolan would have tried the whirlpool bath to help himself relax, maybe inviting Beacher in to join him for a while. But these weren't other circumstances, and the honeymoon he'd joked about had never started.

They were on a mission that was bound to end in blood, and Bolan spent the next ten minutes washing off old stains, wishing the hot water and soap could reach his conscience and his soul.

"IT FIGURES we'd get stuck with this," Colin MacGregor groused. "Out on the feckin' boat all day, and now we hafta go around askin' about more feckin' boats."

"The old kraut's paranoid," Jimmy Raeburn said, talking from the left side of his mouth while fussing with a match to light his cigarette. "He sees a boat pass on the loch and makes it some kinda conspiracy."

"He likely thinks it's the Israelis," MacGregor said, "come to lift him for a trial back home."

"Like anyone remembers the old shite's alive, or gives a damn," Raeburn replied.

"Macauley seems to set a lotta store by him," MacGregor said.

"And who's Macauley, when you think about it?" Raeburn asked. "Just another fat-arse, la-di-da *aristocrat* tellin' the little people where to go and what to do. I dunno why Fergus coddles him."

"The money, eh? Why else?" MacGregor said.

"What else," Raeburn echoed, sounding resigned and disappointed all at once.

They'd found three places listed in the Fort Augustus telephone directory where small boats were available for hire. The first was closed when they arrived, and an old lady in the shop next door told Raeburn that its owner was in the hospital. Something about his back that didn't mean a damn to Raeburn, so he stopped listening.

The second place was open, but it rented only kayaks and canoes, cheaper to buy and to maintain, without a single moving part, and certain tourists seemed to like that kind of thing. The woman who'd been left in charge was easy on the eyes and all, but Raeburn didn't have the time to flirt with her.

"Third time's a charm," MacGregor said.

"I bloody well hope so," Raeburn replied.

MacGregor was right, up to a point.

Their third stop had the kind of motorboats Gibson had sent them out to find, all right, and it was situated on the channel where the local tour boat docked, for easy access to the town. A surly codger saw them coming and called out before they reached him, "Too late. There's no more hires today."

"We didn't come to hire a boat," MacGregor said, as they drew closer.

"Makes it easy, then," the man said dismissively.

"We're after information," Raeburn said.

"Across the bridge and on your left, behind the BP station there. I reckon they'll be shut by now. Come back tomorrow after nine."

"Not bloody *tourist* information," MacGregor stated. "What we need to know is who's been hirin' out yer wee boats here."

"Whoever's got the money," the man said, drawing up to his full height of five foot three or four. "And what the hell is it to you?"

"Listen, old man—"

Raeburn saw it was getting out of hand and knew that Gibson would be pissed if they did anything to draw heat from the police. Bad enough that bloody Dengler thought someone was spying on them from the loch, without a constable arriving on Macauley's doorstep.

"Easy, now," he said, more to MacGregor than the old guy, since he figured his colleague was more likely to go off. "We's only come to talk, is all. There might be somethin' in it for ya, if you got the wherewithal to help us."

"Somethin', eh?" the man said. "What kinda somethin'?"

"How's twenty pounds?"

"Depends on what you're askin'. If it's about my customers, fifty'd suit me better."

"Call it fifty, then," Raeburn replied. "If you can help us."

"Ask yer questions," the man said.

"Earlier today, around five o'clock or so, we think you hired a boat out to a tourist type," Raeburn said.

"Haven't heard a question yet."

"Well, *did* you?" MacGregor asked.

"I did."

"You get his name?" Raeburn asked.

"No. Got a deposit on the boat, in case he never brought 'er back. Paid back the half of it when he come in on time."

"He leave you with a name and all to trace him by?" Raeburn asked.

"His pound notes was enough on that score," the man said.

"You're not big on curiosity, I reckon," MacGregor said.

"Not like you lot."

"You can describe him, though, I figure. Just in case he skipped out with your wee boat," Raeburn said.

"Six foot, I'd say, and call it fourteen stones. Dark hair, clean shaved. He wasn't local. Sounded like a Yank to me, no British in his voice at all."

"You see him with a car?" MacGregor asked.

The man shook his head. "Nobody parks down here except the registrar and water bailiff. He'd have used the car park up the road, or left it somewhere else."

"You reckon he was police?" Raeburn asked.

The man thought about it, then shook his head. "He had a smell, I don't deny it. But he weren't from the constabulary."

"And there's nothing else?" Raeburn asked.

"Just my fifty pounds," the man said. "Don't be forgettin' that."

AFTER THE BEST MEAL that he'd had in weeks—smoked salmon, followed by prime rib with roast potatoes, garden vegetables and a sweet horseradish sauce—Bolan went back up to the room and waited while Beacher changed into what she called her working clothes—gray jacket, with coordinated blouse and slacks, and sturdy flats replacing the high heels she'd worn to dinner. Once she'd tied her hair back, she was ready for the road.

Full night had fallen by the time they stepped into the Inchnacardoch's parking lot. A floodlight helped them find the Camry, and the driveway was illuminated, but Beacher had told him that the road they would be traveling was dark and narrow, prone to accidents if someone took the two-lane track too fast, or with a little too much whisky underneath his or her belt.

Bolan drove back through Fort Augustus, following Beacher's directions and a small sign for the B862. Off to his left, the former abbey showed warm lights in many of its windows, indicating that the guests had settled in. Beyond it, Bolan drove through trees and watched for stray sheep, crossed a stone bridge wide enough for one car at a time, and then picked up his speed a bit, swinging around the south end of Loch Ness.

Chasing the twin beams of his headlights through the night, he could imagine how the early settlers had to have felt, huddled in thatch-roofed huts along the loch's shore, sharing stories of a beast that rose by night to claim their cattle, or to snatch a careless traveler. He understood how superstition could take root, perhaps encouraging reports of sightings in broad daylight.

Or, there might be something in the dark loch after all.

When the highway split again, a mile or so from Fort Augustus, Bolan stayed with the Glendoe Road. His other choice, Beacher explained, would take them to the Glendoe Lodge, then snake around through hills until it came lochside with a dead end. To reach Macauley's property, they had to take the relatively long way round, past Glendoebeg, Loch Tarff, and on across the windy moors, until the B852 branched off, half a mile due south of Bailebeag.

So Bolan stayed the course, seeing no more of the surrounding countryside than high beams would allow, surprised at intervals by sheep whose rumps were spray-painted in garish shades of pink and green.

"What's with the colored sheep?" he asked.

"The farmers here use paint, instead of brands," Beacher replied. "It's more humane and washes out at shearing time."

Thus educated, Bolan made his turn onto the B852 as scheduled, hardly surprised to see the road grow narrower as he departed from the main highway. Two cars could still pass each other, traveling in opposite directions, but if either driver let his or her eyes or attention wander, paint and wing mirrors would be lost.

"Macauley's land begins about two miles ahead," Beacher advised. "Before we get to Boleskine House."

"I've heard of that," Bolan remarked. "Can't place it, though."

"Aleister Crowley lived there for a dozen years or so, until the eve of World War I," Beacher explained. "The witchy fellow. Liked to call himself the Great Beast. He later died from heroin, and Jimmy Page moved in. You'll know him as the lead guitarist from Led Zeppelin. It looks across a cemetery to the loch."

"Charming."

"We won't be stopping in," she said. "But if I had a choice, I'd rather share a dram with Crowley than our Alastair Macauley."

"I don't think he'll be inviting us for tea," Bolan replied.

"Let's hope not, anyhow."

Five minutes later, Beacher said, "All right, this is his property, off to our left. The main gate should be coming up... right...now."

Bolan slowed to give himself a better look. The tall gate was wrought iron anchored to tall stone pillars, with a fence stretching away in each direction, topped by decorative spear points. Bolan couldn't tell how sharp they were in passing, but he guessed they weren't entirely there for show.

"Man likes his privacy," he said.

"He does, indeed. You saw the cameras above the gate?"

"I did," Bolan replied. "One for visitors, the other turned out toward the road. I couldn't tell if it was tracking."

"New technology for the old laird," Beacher observed with just a hint of sarcasm.

"I'd like to make another pass," Bolan said, "if we find a place where I can turn around."

"I told you, it'll have to be a private driveway. If we... What?"

Headlights appeared behind them, emerging from Macauley's gate and following.

"We've either got a tail," Bolan replied, "or someone's got a sudden urge to take a moonlight drive."

Beacher turned in her seat and said, "I don't like the way this feels."

"Okay," Bolan replied. "Let's find out if they're serious."

10

"They's runnin'," Raeburn said.

"I see that," MacGregor answered, sounding snippish as he jammed down the pedal and powered after the Toyota they'd scrambled to pursue.

The two had been on guard duty until midnight, after all they'd done that day already, for the laird and Gibson. Raeburn knew when he was getting hosed, but what was he supposed to do about it? Any luck, they would've caught four hours' sleep, but with this latest development he knew there'd be no end of work to do, no matter how it went.

They had the laird's Mercedes—make that *one* of them, the S-Class W221 Saloon. Macauley seemed to have a fleet of them.

"C'mon," he urged MacGregor at the wheel. "Close up with 'em."

"This isn't the motorway," MacGregor replied. "I'm doin' what I can."

In fact, Raeburn knew that the smaller car in front of them had an advantage on the B852. The Mercedes might have more power for an all-out hammer down the open straightaway, but narrow lochside roads were something else. You never knew when you would meet a truck or a tractor, find a flock of sheep crossing the road, or hit a rockslide when you least expected it. A smaller car might slip around or through some obstacle, leaving the Benz to crash and burn.

Which Raeburn wouldn't mind if he was just a spectator, but as it was…

"What model's that?" MacGregor asked, as if it made a bit of difference.

"Dunno," Raeburn replied.

"The bastard can drive," MacGregor said. "I give him that."

"Give him a bit more gas, why don't ya, and let's get this done."

They both had pistols, Raeburn's being a Swiss SIG-Sauer P-239. He had two spare magazines, which gave him thirty shots, and he was also carrying their big gun for the evening, a Remington 870 pump-action shotgun with eight rounds of buckshot in its magazine.

Not that he planned on shooting anyone, he thought. Their orders were to follow and observe the suspect car, but when the Toyota took off at speed, running them down became the only option. Any idiot knew the other driver wouldn't lead them back to his hotel, once he'd seen that he was being tailed. And with the day he'd had already, Raeburn didn't want to think about the damned tongue lashing he'd receive from Gibson if he came back empty-handed.

So, they had to catch the cheeky bugger and find out who in hell he was. Depending on how *that* went, Raeburn would decide what happened next. A local wouldn't run that way nor should a tourist out to put some mileage on his rental car after dark. That meant a guilty conscience, Raeburn figured, and fear of being caught.

But who? And why?

"We're losin' 'em," he warned MacGregor.

"Och, gimme some credit, will you?" the driver answered, pouring on more speed from somewhere, narrowing the gap.

Raeburn had heard about the shoot-up down in Glasgow, but he couldn't quote chapter and verse about the city gangs. A thousand people had to hate Frankie Boyle, but how did that connect to someone shadowing Macauley's place—and possibly the research boat, as well?

Questions. And he'd have answers, once they'd stopped the runner and found out what he wanted, who he worked for, what he knew about Macauley working with the TIF.

Ask him about the loch, while they were at it. Sure.

But first, they obviously had to catch him.

"Faster, Colin! Jesus! If he gets to Inverfarigaig, we'll lose him to the police."

"And suppose he *is* the police, eh?" MacGregor replied. "What then?"

"Just drive," Raeburn replied. "I'll do the thinkin', shall I?"

MacGregor muttered something unintelligible, and they raced on through the night.

"THEY'RE HANGING IN," Bolan advised Beacher. "The wheel-man knows his business."

"Worse luck for us," she said, still half-turned in her seat to watch the headlights coming up behind them. She had her Glock in hand, index finger straight beside the trigger guard.

Bolan could think of worse places to stage a running fire-fight, but the lochside road was bad enough. It was narrow and sinuous, with nowhere to stand and fight that wasn't on or near civilian private property. With Britain's strict controls on firearms, gunshots in the middle of the night were sure to prompt a flurry of alerts to the police.

Where would they come from, then? And how long would it take them to arrive?

Beacher had pegged the Fort Augustus station as a two-man shop, which meant twelve-hour shifts with one on duty and the other off at home or somewhere else. Beacher wasn't sure about the town of Inverfarigaig, ahead of them. No clue as to its size or population, whether there would be another station there, but Bolan doubted it. There would be cops to spare in Inverness, but that was forty minutes farther north, at least, once they were notified and en route with sirens bleating.

So, they didn't have to worry about getting busted in the short term, but he dreaded pulling one or two unseasoned constables into the middle of a shootout where the other side might feel no hesitation in eliminating them. Bolan had no idea if rural stations kept a weapon in the house for dire emergencies, but most cops in the UK were unarmed, and thus doubly at risk from any unexpected clash with terrorists.

"I have a thought," Beacher advised him, "but you may not like it."

"Go," Bolan replied.

"All right. I've changed my mind about a stop at Boleskine House."

"Explain."

"It's vacant, and it gets us off the highway," she replied. "We'll be a quarter mile or more from any neighbors, buffered by the hills and forest."

"Lead them down there," Bolan said, thinking aloud, "and show them some black magic."

"If we're doing it," she said, "the turnoff is about a thousand yards up ahead, and on our left."

Procrastination wasn't one of Bolan's weaknesses. He made the choice and saw the left turn coming at them in his high beams, slowed enough to make it with the rubber squealing underneath them, then he powered through a short dogleg and found another road that took them back in the direction they had come from, running parallel to the B852.

"There'll be another turnoff to your right," Beacher said. "Watch for it within a quarter mile."

"Will do."

And if they missed the turn to Boleskine House, the map in Bolan's head told him they would keep rolling down the east shore of Loch Ness to pass a large fish hatchery, then a waste treatment plant, before they hit a cul-de-sac at lochside and were trapped.

No good.

It was the Great Beast's former home or nothing, if they meant to keep the scuffle relatively quiet and away from prying eyes. If they survived, there would be time to think about disposal of the losers and their vehicle, any touch-ups the Camry might require, or even ditching it to hire another ride in Inverness. The best way to approach successive crises was by dealing with one problem at a time.

Survival first. If they could pull that off, the rest would follow naturally. And if they had a chance to question Macauley's men, so much the better.

But he wasn't counting on it.

The pursuit was shaping up to be a rumble, and in most such situations, only one side walked away.

If that.

He saw the access road to Boleskine House, working the brake and gas in tandem as he made the turn.

"Be ready," Bolan told Beacher. "We only have one chance to do this right."

MY FAULT, Beacher thought, as they roared into the turn and swooped downhill toward Boleskine House. A cemetery flashed past in their headlight beams, its mossy headstones ranked like dwarfish soldiers in the darkness, there and gone almost before they registered.

As soon as Cooper accepted her idea, Beacher had felt a surge of second thoughts. But he was turning then, leaving the B852, with their pursuers coming up behind. She couldn't take it back, confess her own misgivings when he needed only strength from her, and fortitude.

It meant more killing when they stopped, unless the people who were chasing them decided to surrender, and she didn't see that happening. Whether the hunters were Macauley's men or hard-core TIF—or both—she knew they would be under orders to identify their quarry and eliminate them, if they posed a threat.

So be it.

She'd signed on for this with eyes wide-open, as had her superiors. If anything went wrong, built-in deniability would leave Beacher holding the bag and taking full responsibility for any violations of procedure. She would certainly be sacked, and likely prosecuted in the bargain. Twenty years in Cornton Vail, the Scottish women's prison, ought to get her out of sight and out of mind.

On the other hand, if she and Cooper succeeded…then, what? There could be no public recognition or reward, only a shifting of responsibility to blame the fallen for their own demise.

At least the government was fairly good at that, she thought.

A heartbeat later, they were rolling past tall hedges at the entrance to a kind of courtyard, headlight beams sweeping a house with vacant, darkened windows as expected. Anyone who met them here would be a squatter or a ghost, and Beacher had no fear of either.

"Be ready to bail," Bolan said, as he kept driving, on around the south end of the long, low house to put the Camry out of sight. However briefly, it would add confusion to the mix and possibly protect the car from damage.

When he braked, Beacher was out and moving with her Glock in hand, retracing their path toward the front of the house. Cooper was a little slower, she noticed, opening the Camry's trunk and rummaging inside one of the bags he had secreted there. She heard a clank of gunmetal and wondered what he had in store for their pursuers.

Then the other car was coming, revving down the curved driveway, then slowing when its high beams showed no vehicle in front of Boleskine House. If these were local drivers, they would likely know the layout of the grounds; if not, they might suspect that they had missed a hidden turnoff, maybe lost their quarry somewhere in the twists and turns of leaving the B852 behind.

Delay was good. It let Cooper join her while the chase car idled in the driveway, then began to creep in closer, moving at a crawl. The big American carried some kind of assault rifle. Her mind clicked in a second later, with the ID on a Steyr AUG.

"I wasn't in the Girl Guides," he advised her, "but I like to be prepared myself."

"They're undecided," Beacher whispered to him, standing in the shadow of a house known for black magic and dark deeds.

"I won't mind if they turn around," he said. "If we have to take the long way home, it's better than a premature firefight."

Beacher was wondering if their pursuers had the Camry's license number, or were smart and well-equipped enough to trace it. If they did and could, they would have Cooper's ID— for whatever that might be worth. Where they might go from there was anybody's—

"Here they come," he said.

The chase car rumbled toward the porch of Boleskine House.

"YOU RECOGNIZE this place?" Raeburn asked.

"Why the hell should I?" MacGregor replied.

"Jaysus, you're ignorant. You didn't even see the sign we passed just now?"

"Somethin' about a mole," MacGregor said.

"Not mole, *bole*. This is Boleskine House!"

"Is that suppose to mean somethin'?" MacGregor asked.

Raeburn could only shake his head in awe at the deficiency of his partner's education. Next, he'd claim he never heard of Irn-Bru or Tennent's Lager.

"It's the Devil's house," Raeburn said. "Did ya never learn that as a child?"

"Devil my arse," MacGregor scoffed. "Just tell me if ya see that damned Toyota."

"Nothin' yet," Raeburn replied, clutching his shotgun in a stranglehold that made his knuckles ache.

"I'm goin' in," MacGregor said, lifting off the brake, letting the Benz coast the remainder of the way into the courtyard with its engine barely idling. Even so, it seemed hellishly loud to Raeburn, riding with his window down and peering past their headlight beams into the darkness.

"Think we coulda missed 'em?" Raeburn asked, hating the hopeful tone he heard in his own voice.

"On that road?" MacGregor answered. "Not unless they beamed up, Scotty."

They were rolling closer to the bulk of Boleskine House, a yard at a time. Raeburn turned in his seat and eased the muzzle of his shotgun out the window, covering the south end of the structure more or less.

"They musta pulled around in back," MacGregor said, and turned the Benz in that direction, still not giving it much gas. Their headlights swept across the house's long facade, making the windows seem to wink at them like knowing eyes.

"If they's inside the house—" Raeburn began, but never had a chance to finish as the dark night came alive with muzzle-flashes. The Mercedes started taking hits, and while he fired a shotgun blast in answer, he was more concerned with ducking below the line of fire.

Too late. The windshield popped, then shattered into pebbles as the safety glass imploded. Raeburn heard MacGregor's cry of pain but didn't check to see how badly he was hit. If dead or dying, he was already beyond his help. If not...well, he could damn well look out for himself.

As Raeburn meant to do.

He spilled out of the car's passenger side, cursing the dome light that exposed him to his enemies, and hit the pavement hard on his left shoulder, rolling awkwardly away as the Mercedes grumbled on without him. Raeburn heard slugs breaking glass and punching rude holes in the Benz's body. Somewhere in the middle of it, MacGregor revved the engine and began returning fire with his handgun.

Which covered Raeburn as he scuttled toward the shadow of Boleskine House. It wasn't much, in terms of sanctuary, but he'd damn well take what he could get.

The driveway's gravel hurt his palms and knees, but it was better than a bullet in the gut. Raeburn crept closer to the house, watching the Benz absorb its punishment, dome light still burning over MacGregor's slack and bloody form, until the car collided with a hedge and stalled.

They'd come hunting him next, he knew. Even if they had missed him bailing out, they had to see the open door and grasp its obvious significance. Two guns, at least, and one of them an automatic shooter, damn it.

But if he could find them first…

The best defense was still a good offense, whoever said it. Rising from his knees and taking baby steps to keep the gravel quiet, Raeburn went to find his enemies.

"There's still one," Bolan said. "I saw him bail."

"He may be running," Beacher whispered back.

Bolan stood listening, his ears still echoing with gunfire, while the stalled Mercedes engine ticked and cooled. He heard no sound of running feet on gravel, nothing like a body pushing through the hedges that surrounded Boleskine House, but he supposed the second shooter might have found a place to hide.

"We can't leave him behind," he told Beacher.

Or even drive out safely, with a gunman crouching somewhere in the shadows. If he wasn't wounded, wasn't terrified, he'd have the perfect opportunity to ambush them.

And leaving him alive increased the chance that they would be identified before Bolan was ready to reveal his hand.

"So," Beacher answered, "do you want the front or back?"

It had become a lethal game of hide-and-seek, not Bolan's favorite, but he had played it many times before, prevailing with a mix of stealth and ruthlessness.

"Front," Bolan answered, guessing that the second shooter hadn't traveled far in the few seconds since he'd leaped out of the battered Benz. Whether he'd try to creep around the house and take them from the rear was anybody's guess, but Beacher could prevent him getting to the Camry, leaving them on foot.

They separated then, and Bolan eased his way around the southwest corner of the house. Across the sloping lawn, through treetops, he could see Loch Ness with moonlight on the water, but he had no time to stop and look for monsters rising from its depths.

A real-world danger occupied his full attention.

Clearing the corner, Bolan found a strip of grass and soil to walk on at the driveway's edge, clearing the gravel. Behind him, he could hear a dripping sound from the Mercedes, maybe fluid from the punctured radiator or—

A *whump* corrected that impression, as the leakage from a broken fuel line found hot metal, sparked and spread. Bolan was dropping to a crouch when flames blossomed behind him and the yard of Boleskine House was suddenly illuminated.

In front of him, the second shooter wore a shocked expression on his pale face, muttered something that was probably a curse and swung a shotgun into line.

Bolan was faster, triggering a 3-round burst of 5.56 mm manglers at a range of twenty feet or less. The standing figure took all three and toppled over backward with a wheezing sound from ruptured lungs. Too late, he found the shotgun's trigger and dispatched a blast of buckshot toward the sky.

Beacher came running from behind the house, pistol extended, lowering the piece when she saw Bolan on his feet beside a corpse. "That's it, then?" she inquired.

"Looks like it," Bolan said.

Eyeing the Benz, she said, "You want to put that out before it blows?"

"We may as well," Bolan replied.

She disappeared again and came back from the Camry moments later with a tire iron and a fire extinguisher. Bolan relieved her of the iron and used it on the Benz's hood to spare his hands from scorching. Once he had it open, Beacher foamed the engine down with the extinguisher and left it steaming in the night.

"My good deed for the day," she said.

"No need to burn a piece of history," Bolan said, as he turned away.

Back in the Camry, Beacher said, "They'll have something to think about, at least. Whatever they've been doing on the loch, maybe they'll hurry up."

And start to make mistakes, Bolan thought, though he couldn't count on that.

"They're after something," he replied. "If we knew what it was, we'd be a long way toward the wrap-up."

"Well, we can't exactly ask," she said.

"Maybe we can," Bolan replied.

"How's that?" she asked.

"I'll have to think about it. First, I want to get a look behind Macauley's walls."

"Now that he's looking out for trouble?"

"It's a problem I can work around," he told her.

"Not tonight?" She sounded worried.

"No," he said. "We'll let them stew a bit. Tomorrow, after breakfast, when his crew's out on the loch."

"Broad daylight, then." She wasn't pleased.

"The better to see all his secrets," Bolan said.

11

"The laird's awake," Ewan MacKinnon told the men who waited in the combination den and trophy room. "He'll be down soon."

Gibson watched the ghillie leave and close the door behind him, letting several seconds more slip past before he spoke. "They're either dead," he told the others, "or they'll bloody wish they were when I get through with them."

"Maybe they ran into the police," Wallace said. "Them having guns and all. They could be sittin' there in Fort Augustus, or gone up to Inverness for questioning."

"They would've called us, don't you think? It's going on nine hours since they left, for feck's sake. You could drive to John of Groats and back in that time, with a meal and stop for petrol on the way."

The old man in the wheelchair cleared his throat, a rattling sound that never failed to set Gibson's teeth on edge. Sometimes the loathsome noise preceded speech; at other times, it was a simple complement to breathing at the age of ninety-something, winding up a misspent life.

This time, the wizened figure spoke.

"We must accept that they are dead," he told Gibson and Wallace, showing no emotion. "It remains to learn how they were killed, by whom, and what it means for us."

"Beyond losing two friends, you mean?" Wallace asked, bristling.

"It is foolish to make friends in wartime. Soldiers are expendable, you realize?"

Wallace was turning red when Gibson interrupted him. "He's right, Graham. They went out armed to do a job, and bein' gone this long tells me they failed. We need to be thinkin' of damage control."

"And what you tell the laird, *ja?* He will not be happy when the police find guns and dead men in his pretty car, eh? Many questions will be asked."

"Jaysus!" Gibson was mortified he hadn't thought of that. A sleepless night had left him groggy, prone to making grave mistakes. "We need to get in front of this," he told Wallace.

"How's that suppose to work?" Graham replied.

"Call the police at once," the old man said. "Tell them you just noticed the car is missing. Thieves must have come in and taken it last night."

"Thieves came in through the gate?" Wallace replied. "You reckon they'll believe that shite?"

"You left the gate open," the old man said. "It was a foolish thing to do. Perhaps you were drinking, eh?"

"So it's on me, is it?"

"A simple error," the old man said. "Would you rather be embarrassed, or in prison?"

"Do it, Graham," Gibson ordered. "Make the call."

Fumbling for his cell phone, Wallace asked them, "What about the boys, then? What am I suppose to tell the police about them?"

The old man spread his liver-spotted hands, palms raised, as if it should be obvious. "They are the thieves," he said. "Perhaps the car was to be used in robbery. Who knows?"

"Stolen by men who work for us?"

"Who knows this? Who can prove it?" the old man asked. "Keep your wits about you and be calm."

Scowling, Wallace moved off into a corner of the den and faced the wall as he dialed 999. A moment later, Gibson heard him muttering in conversation with the operator, who'd inquire as to the nature of his personal emergency and patch him through to the appropriate connection.

"You still have an unpleasant task before you," the old man told Gibson.

"Right. The laird."

"The good news is that he still requires your services. If he dismisses you, he must begin the search again from scratch."

"He might do that, if we bring police to his doorstep," Gibson worried.

"*Nein*. He is a true believer in your cause, Herr Gibson."

"Yeah? Well that explains him, then. But what about yourself, eh?"

"You know the proverb, the enemy of my enemy is my friend."

"So, who's your enemy, again?"

"Today," the old man said, "it is the same as yours."

"England. I thought as much," Gibson said.

"We are two unlikely allies, I admit," the German said. "You may be pleased to know that our collaboration will be brief. *Schriftsatz*."

"Meaning, because you're old?"

"It's undeniable," the wizened figure told him, smiling with a set of high-priced dentures. "I have survived this long, when all my friends fell, to strike a final blow. Do you believe in destiny?"

"I'm trying to," Gibson replied.

Wallace was coming back to them, closing his phone. "It's done," he said. "One of 'em's comin' out to look around and ask his questions. Should be here within the hour."

"So, we've got our story straight, then?" Gibson asked him.

But before Wallace could answer, Macauley entered. He was wearing tweed, as usual, together with his normal frown.

"Good morning, gentlemen," he said, then seemed to read their mood. The frown deepened as he inquired, "What's wrong?"

BACK AT THE LODGE, Bolan and Beacher were awake by half-past five, checking the television news, but most of it came out of London, via BBC. The Scottish channel—STV—had weather, sports, some politics, a teenage hiker's rape and murder outside Aviemore, but nothing on the shooting of two TIF commandos at Loch Ness.

"Looks like they missed it," Beacher said.

"That kind of luck can't hold," Bolan replied. "Assume they took one of Macauley's cars. He'll have to think about what happens next, whether they're found this morning or a year from now. The guns raise questions he can't answer honestly. He'll need a cover story."

"So, you're thinking he'll report it?"

"Or have someone on his payroll do it," Bolan answered. "Not the shooting. If he knows about that, he could try to sanitize the scene. But if he only knows his car and men are missing—"

"He'll report a theft," Beacher finished his thought. "Of course."

"It's what I'd do," Bolan said. "Buy some time while he's erasing any links between himself and two dead shooters."

"And he's hunting us in the meantime," she said.

"Not us, specifically. But someone, sure."

"That doesn't trouble you?" she asked.

"He doesn't know us," Bolan said, "or where to find us. We have the advantage."

"But—"

His cell phone interrupted her, a shiver on his hip. Bolan said, "Hold that thought" and answered it, to find a photo on the LED screen. He was looking at the old man from Macauley's dock, in what may well have been a passport photo. Next up was a candid photo of the same man, decades younger, in a military uniform. The silver death's-head on his black peaked cap identified him as a member of Adolf Hitler's so-called "elite" SS. Bolan didn't recognize rank depicted by the oak leaves on his collar, but he showed Beacher the photographs, then scrolled past to the text from Stony Man Farm.

"He's Jurgen Otto Dengler," Bolan told her, summarizing. "Formerly Standartenführer—the equivalent of colonel—in the old SS. Born August 13, 1913, in Bavaria."

"My God," she said. "He's ancient."

"Joined the Nazi Party on his eighteenth birthday, 1931, and graduated to the SS two years later. Came up through the ranks by 1940 to work with something called the *Sonderkommando Kuensberg,* one of the looting units that started in France, then shifted to Russia in 1941. Sought for war crimes after VE-Day, but the ODESSA network helped him slip through Spain to South America. Apparently, he lives in Switzerland these days."

"Except when he's in Scotland," Beacher said. "And he is here because…?"

"No word on that," Bolan replied. "Officially, he's wanted by Mossad and Interpol, but no one's really looking for him. Age and all the Swiss red tape have given him a pass."

"A Nazi colonel with a looting unit," Beacher said. "I see how he'd wind up in Switzerland. He's probably got gold and jewels and God knows what else stashed in vaults and decorating some chalet. But why risk coming out to hobnob with the TIF? And why Loch Ness?"

"We ought to ask him," Bolan said.

"I doubt he's granting interviews," Beacher replied.

"Something could be arranged."

"You're set on dropping in to see the laird, then."

"Can you think of an alternative?" Bolan asked.

"I'm still working on it. Give me time."

"We don't have much to spare," he said. "Whatever Dengler and Macauley hope to find, it stands to benefit the TIF, otherwise Gibson and his people wouldn't be involved. If we don't stay on top of it, it could slip through our fingers."

"But what *is* it?" Beacher challenged him. "Some kind of

Nazi secret weapon from the forties? It would be a rusted-out antique by now."

"Dengler wasn't a weapons guy," Bolan replied. "He was a looter. Probably a murderer, on top of it, but basically a thief. Thieves steal. We know that tons of Nazi loot has never been recovered."

"Right," Beacher agreed. "In Zurich or wherever Dengler hangs his hat. Maybe in Paraguay or Argentina. But the Highlands?"

"One more thing to ask about, if we can get our hands on someone from Macauley's camp."

"We're going back, then," Beacher said, sounding resigned.

"But after breakfast," Bolan said. "I need a little something for the road."

WALLACE WAS DISTRACTED as the *DeepScan* chugged its way past Urquhart Castle's ruined battlements, northbound. There were no tourists at the castle yet since it was only just past 7:30 a.m. His thoughts went to ancient days when quarrels were settled with swords and axes, hand to hand.

People were still dying around Loch Ness, it seemed—but these days they disappeared, as well.

He tried to imagine what had become of Colin MacGregor and Jimmy the Cat Raeburn, but it didn't compute. They'd gone to tail a car that had made Gibson suspicious, and they'd never made it back. So...what?

Wallace assumed both men were dead. There was no reason in the world that he could think of for the two of them to leave without a parting word, much less to steal the laird's Mercedes-Benz. Somehow, they'd stumbled into deadly trouble without calling to report.

And then?

Whoever killed them hadn't left them sitting on the roadside in Macauley's car. Because that would have been too obvious, perhaps? Or was the disappearing act part of some larger strategy? And if so, to what aim?

Police killed people, sure, though it was fairly rare in the UK. Wallace had never heard of coppers making anybody disappear after they'd killed him, though. That was a gangster kind of deal, or something spies might do.

The thought of gangsters led him back to Frankie Boyle, steaming in Glasgow over recent losses and the termination of his contract to provide arms for the TIF. Would Boyle send someone north to get a little payback? Wallace hadn't thought of it last night, and couldn't put it on the radio to Gibson at the manor house, but when they made it back to shore that afternoon he'd definitely float the possibility.

And if it wasn't Boyle...then he was back to zero. No feckin' clue, he thought in frustration, to help him solve the riddle that was haunting him.

He'd left before the police reached Macauley's place that morning. With MacGregor and Raeburn missing, he'd tapped a couple other boys to help him man the *DeepScan,* Danny Bain and Alfie Drever. That left four men at the house with Gibson and the laird, disguised as workmen, and he'd given thought to calling reinforcements, but it might look bád, with the law sniffing around.

It was a tough call, whether he should hope the police found MacGregor and Raeburn, or they didn't. Wallace didn't care for unsolved mysteries, but if the men—make that their bodies—were discovered, it would only raise more questions. At the moment, local constables would be concerned about a rich man's stolen car. But if they found the Benz with guns and bodies in it, it would mean involving CID inspectors, maybe even MI-5.

No good could come of that. It wouldn't take the big boys long to suss out Laird Macauley's tie-in to the Tartan Independence Front, and once that information got around it would be every hapless bastard for himself, he figured. The end of everything, most likely. Living underground. The money tap shut off. No guns from Frankie Boyle.

In his frustration, Wallace felt a surge of anger against

Raeburn and MacGregor. Miserable idiots running off to God knew where and getting killed, with no thought for the trouble it would bring to everybody else around them. Wallace would've liked to kill them both himself, for that, but as it was he simply clenched his fists and watched the hulk of Urquhart Castle pass on their port side.

His mind was drifting when he heard a shout from Danny Bain, belowdecks. "Graham!" Bain hailed him. "Come'n have a look at this, then!"

Wallace found Bain at his place before the *DeepScan*'s several color monitors. As he approached, Bain pointed at something on the screen connected to the seabed scanner.

"What's that, then, do ya reckon?" Bain asked him.

Wallace leaned in close to get a better look. He understood enough about the gear to judge the size of most objects displayed, ranging from fish to sunken logs and rowboats. This thing was roughly torpedo-shaped and lay at rest on the bed of Loch Ness. If Wallace was reading the monitor's scale correctly, the object measured... Jaysus, he thought, could that be right? More than two hundred feet from end to end?

It could. It was.

"Is that the monster, then?" Bain asked Danny.

"Better," Wallace replied.

He left Bain perched before the monitors and hurried back to the companionway, then up the metal steps to reach the wheelhouse. Henry Bell half turned to face him, sitting on a swivel seat with one hand on the *DeepScan*'s wheel.

"You seen a ghost, or what?" he asked Wallace.

"I've seen the future," Wallace told him. "Hold 'er here, while I raise Fergus at the big house."

"Aye," Bell said, rising to draw the throttle levers back and leave the engines idling down below.

Wallace knew what to say, the message he had to send announcing contact, without giving anything away on-air, where hostiles might be listening.

"*DeepScan* to base," he said into the microphone, surprised to hear the tremor in his voice. "*DeepScan* to base. We have contact."

DAYLIGHT MADE a world of difference, evoking brilliant colors as the Camry rolled through Fort Augustus, past the Highland Club, and off along the B862 around the south tip of Loch Ness at about 8:30 a.m. At first, a range of greens predominated, then a world of browns and grays took over on the moors, with purple sprays of heather visible along both sides. There were more sheep in evidence, joined here and there by brindled Highland cattle or Aberdeen Angus.

"I still think this is risky," Beacher said, as they approached Loch Tarff, winding along its eastern shore with close to zero visibility on looping turns.

"You're right," Bolan agreed. "But every move we make up here is risky. We've got tourist creds established, with the hotel and the marriage cover. Strangers drive all over here throughout the season. It's the best that we can do."

"I could have checked with the police," she said.

"And asked them what? 'Have you found any corpses since last night, in a Mercedes?'"

"I'd have tried to be a bit more subtle," she replied.

"We've got it covered," Bolan told her. "Boleskine House is famous. It's on every tourist map they sell in Fort Augustus. Driving by won't make us suspects."

"But we're *only* driving by," she emphasized.

"That's right. Then heading back up country to Macauley's spread."

"There's still no way that I can talk you out of that?" she asked.

"The *DeepScan*'s working on the loch," Bolan replied. "That's four men from Macauley's staff accounted for, plus two last night. If he's got backup coming in, they should be here this afternoon. I'll never have a better time, with fewer guns on-site."

"And the police? You said someone will likely call them to report Macauley's car missing."

"I'm guessing that they'd phone it in first thing," Bolan said. "With Macauley's bankroll, there'll be no delay in sending someone out to take a statement. Put a 'be on the lookout' on the Benz, and that's a wrap."

"Until they find it," Beacher said.

He nodded. "Right."

"And when they do?" she prodded.

"Cops identify the shooters, if they're in the system. That should turn a spotlight on the TIF, and maybe on Macauley."

"I doubt the CID could get a search warrant from that, much less permission to arrest Macauley."

"Is that what you want?" Bolan inquired.

She frowned and said, "I want him out of action."

"Right," he said, and let it go at that.

They drove through Whitebridge, eight miles out from Fort Augustus. Bolan's guidebook told him that the village claimed a hundred residents, living within a five-mile radius of small shops and the picturesque Whitebridge Hotel. The year-round residents who aren't involved in farming drove to work each day in Inverness, a fifty-mile round-trip commute.

Another two miles up the road, he signaled for the turn-off to the B852 and followed it the same as last time, to the left-hand jog that led them back toward Boleskine House. Beacher's tension was palpable, but Bolan put it out of mind and concentrated on the narrow roads, alert for lay-bys and oncoming vehicles.

A hundred yards before they reached the final turnoff to the sloping drive of Boleskine House, he saw a wrecker rumbling toward them, towing a sedan. Beside him, Beacher stiffened and muttered, "Marvelous."

It was the Benz, complete with shattered windshield, bullet scars and scorch marks on the hood, which had been lowered since they'd left it open after dousing flames beneath it. Bolan observed the car in passing, something any tourist on the road would do, and saw no body in the driver's seat.

"We missed the ambulance," Beacher observed.

"Or else they've laid the bodies out for an examination at the scene," he said.

"The medical examiner's in Inverness," she told him. "So is North Division headquarters for the Scottish Ambulance Service. Calculate arrival time from when the bodies were discovered."

"Doesn't matter," Bolan told her. "Someone heard the shots or noticed something afterward and called it in. If they were driving past, they cleared the road before we left. We're good to go."

"Full speed ahead, then." From her tone, Bolan could tell she wasn't thrilled.

"If you want me to, I'll drop you back in Fort Augustus first. You can arrange for someone to come by and pick you up at the hotel."

"And tell my boss I did a runner halfway through the program? That should put a big smile on his face."

"Might be the best thing for you," Bolan said.

Keeping her eyes fixed on the narrow road ahead, she said, "Forget it, eh? I'm on for the duration."

"Right, then," Bolan said, and motored south toward the waste treatment plant, where zigzag access roads would lead him back to the B852 northbound and Alastair Macauley's mansion on the bluffs above Loch Ness.

12

The damned police were back. It was a bloody inconvenience, most particularly at the present time, but Alastair Macauley was required to deal with them and show at least a modicum of courtesy for individuals so far below his station that their lives could barely be imagined.

Bruce, his longtime butler, led them to the drawing room. This time it was two men in cheap suits off the rack, instead of uniforms. Macauley did not bother looking at the warrant cards they offered for inspection, but he made note of their names: Baikie and Clapperton.

"And how may I assist you, Constables?" Macauley asked.

"Inspectors," Baikie said, correcting him. "We're both with CID. That's the Criminal—"

"I recognize the acronym, of course," Macauley said, cutting him off. "More questions is it, then? About my stolen car?"

"In fact, we've found your car, sir. And a good deal more."

Macauley raised one bristling eyebrow, feigned incomprehension. "Meaning...what, exactly?"

"Corpses, sir," Clapperton said. "Two corpses."

"I'm not sure I understand," Macauley said.

"Are you familiar with a local spot called Boleskine House?" Baikie inquired.

"Of course," Macauley said. "It's well-known. Infamous, in fact."

"And all the more after today, sir," Clapperton advised him.

"It's the place your car was found, shot full of holes and partly burned. There was a dead man in the driver's seat, armed with a pistol. Nearby, on the grounds, we found a second man shot dead. Two guns with that one. It's a double homicide you see, sir."

Time for outrage mingled with confusion. "But I don't… You mean…that is to say…who were these thieves?"

"Thieves, sir?" Baikie was peering at him down a long, thin nose.

"The pair who stole my car," Macauley said to clarify. "Have you identified them?"

Clapperton removed a little notebook from his pocket, opened it and riffled through its pages before answering. "The driver had an operator's license in the name of Colin Reid MacGregor. Do you recognize the name, sir?"

Stupid bastard! Macauley thought. But he said, after consideration, "I do not."

"The other carried no ID," Baikie said. "He was thirty, more or less, with ginger hair and freckles. Something off about his ears, I'd say. Slender, of average height. Do you know anyone who might fit that description, sir?"

"Half of the Highland Scots," Macauley said, "except that funny bit about the ears."

The two inspectors smiled politely at his small bon mot. Clapperton said, "I'm sure that's true, sir. Now, about these guns…"

Macauley echoed, "Guns?" Best to seem ignorant, for the time being.

"The weapons found with these two deaders and your car," Baikie said. "Those would be two semiautomatic pistols, banned under the 1997 *Firearms Act,* and one twelve-bore Remington shotgun lacking proper certification as required under the 1968 *Firearms Act.* Any knowledge of those items, Mr. Macauley?"

"Certainly not," he replied, with just the right measure of bruised dignity.

It was Baikie's turn again. "Aside from those guns—two of which apparently were fired at persons still unknown—the men found with your car were shot with what appears to be a semiautomatic, or perhaps a fully automatic rifle."

"A machine gun, do you mean?" Macauley asked.

"Perhaps, sir," Clapperton replied. "Which would be banned under the 1937 *Firearms Act*. Semiautomatic rifles are proscribed under the *Firearms Act* of 1988. Illegal either way, sir."

"Quite. Well, gentlemen, I wish you both the best of luck in finding those responsible for this atrocity."

"We're thinking, sir," Baikie replied, "that we may be referring this to the Serious Organised Crime Agency. Under the circumstances."

"Absolutely right, too," Macauley said.

"Now, about your car, sir—"

"Sounds like it's a total loss," Macauley said. "I'll need a copy of your constable's report for my insurance carrier, of course."

"Of course, sir," Baikie said. "If you have any further information—"

"You will be the first to know. I won't detain you, now." Macauley pressed a button on the wall to summon Bruce, and watched the CID inspectors leave.

Two stupid bastards dead, he thought, but it would take some time to link him with them, if the police ever did. Meanwhile, Macauley had more pressing matters on his mind.

He had a salvage operation to get started, on the loch.

BOLAN SAW the police car leave Macauley's driveway, watching from concealment in the woods beside the narrow road that passed the laird's estate from Foyers. Beacher had dropped him a half mile beyond, to the south, and gone on in the Camry while Bolan hiked back to his target.

The cops were plainclothes, some kind of detectives, which meant they had been summoned from Inverness after the

Benz and the bodies were found. Macauley would be sweating, worried about exposure of whatever he was doing on the loch and his connection with the Tartan Independence Front, but whether that would slow him was anybody's guess.

The Executioner was skeptical.

In any case, whether the laird backed off or not was beside the point. He had a gang of terrorists employed on some chore at Loch Ness, and breaking off with them—assuming that he even wanted to—would cause more problems than it solved. Smart money said the plot would forge ahead.

All Bolan had to do was find out what the plan involved, then put a stop to it.

Easy as falling off a log.

Into an open grave.

He let the unmarked CID car fade from sight northbound, then rose and moved out toward the fence that ringed Macauley's property. It was a heavy-duty chain-link number—not electrified or fitted with alarms, as Bolan soon discovered—but the spear points he had seen along the highway were replaced inside the forest by an overhanging barbed-wire coil that would make scaling doubly difficult.

No matter. When you couldn't go over, go straight through.

He used wire cutters purchased at the hardware store in Fort Augustus, made himself a gate and wriggled through it, then secured the flap with twist ties bought from the same small shop. The job should pass a casual inspection, from a distance. If someone came by and took a closer look...well, they'd still have to find him on the wooded grounds.

And no one stalked Bolan with impunity.

He knew his relative position to the manor house from satellite images he'd zoomed in on using Beacher's laptop back at the Inchnacardoch Lodge.

Bolan was traveling light on this probe, armed with his Beretta 93-R and the KA-BAR fighting knife, and his sole surveillance tool, the cell phone he had used to photograph the *DeepScan* at Macauley's private dock. He didn't know what to expect, what he might find, but simple logic told him that the laird had secrets he was anxious to conceal—by killing, if it came to that.

A sentient shadow in the forest, Bolan moved out toward the manor house.

"YOU GONNA TELL ME what it is, then?" Danny Bain inquired.

"It's need-to-know," Wallace replied. "Right now, you don't."

"A fine thing that is," Bain groused, but he was used to taking orders. He wouldn't make an issue of it.

They'd completed three more passes in the *DeepScan* of the sunken object since alerting Macauley to their find. It didn't budge an inch from currents at the bottom of the loch, more than six hundred feet below the vessel's keel. The sonar couldn't substitute for underwater cameras, but Wallace knew the object was inanimate. And from his limited research, it measured roughly seven times the length of any so-called monster ever glimpsed by witnesses around Loch Ness—220 feet, or damned close to it by his calculations from the seabed scanner, and some twenty feet in diameter. Off to the port side, a protrusion added ten or eleven feet more at one point, which fit with what he'd been told to expect if the thing had rolled off to one side on impact.

Bloody amazing, that, he thought. To find it after all the time, money and effort that Macauley had invested. Still, he'd only done the easy part so far. Retrieval was another story altogether.

Displacement of the object, spanking new and on the surface, had been registered at 1.56 *million* pounds. Submerged, boost that to 1.77 million. Wallace, trying to imagine all the gear they would require to hoist it from the depths, knew that a ship designed to carry it could never pass along the Caledonian Canal. Toss in the need for secrecy, and raising it was not an option.

More bad news: they would be going deep for salvage,

working at the bottom of the loch where sunlight never reached and any failure of the gear meant instant death. Macauley had a pair of specialists for that, but someone from the TIF contingent would be chosen to accompany them.

Not me, he thought, almost a mantra. Please, not me.

But Wallace knew that he would do as he was told, risk everything as he'd agreed to do when he and Fergus Gibson organized the Tartan Independence Front. He'd known that death was possible when they began.

But Wallace hadn't counted on it happening six hundred feet below the surface of Loch Ness.

WALKING THE LAND and keeping track of what went on there was a basic part of Ewan MacKinnon's routine. As ghillie of Laird Macauley's estate, he was tasked with preserving its wildlife—at least until the big man or his guests were in a killing mood—and protecting the grounds from trespassers. To that end, he inspected every yard of the perimeter each day, unless his duties took him somewhere off the estate—like safeguarding delivery of certain shipments to the manor, for example. Or delivering a token of the laird's displeasure to someone who had offended him.

The latter situation was uncommon. Folks in Foyers, Fort Augustus and environs mostly knew their place. The great majority respected Highland history, tradition and the contributions Macauley had made to the local economy. If he was sometimes abrupt and high-handed, well, what did any Scot expect from minor royalty?

This morning, MacKinnon was checking the estate's perimeter more closely than usual. The previous night's events had riled the laird, not only costing him a pricey vehicle and two men who were scarcely worth their salt, but bringing the police onto his doorstep with their prying questions. That spelled trouble—and it told MacKinnon that the risks of an intrusion had increased.

He didn't know who'd killed the pair of clumsy Lowland-ers, except that those responsible might also threaten Laird Macauley. It was his job to protect the big man and his property against all enemies, whether the adversary was a local poacher or a gun thug up from Glasgow with a score to settle on behalf of Frankie Boyle.

MacKinnon knew about the recent trouble there, and was determined that it wouldn't interfere with Laird Macauley's life or his ongoing work. Particularly when they were so close to ultimate success.

MacKinnon might have missed the flap cut in the fence if he'd been simply walking the perimeter to stretch his legs and get some air. Perhaps. But in defense mode, he was quick to spot the fresh cuts and the twist ties that had been applied to close the makeshift gate. He stopped there, knelt for an inspection of the grass and soil, then turned back toward the manor house with slow, determined strides.

Tracking the enemy.

He knew the way police worked. They'd have come with warrants if they meant to search the place, not sneaking through a hole cut in the fence. The method of approach meant he was dealing with a criminal, or possibly a spy from one of the so-called intelligence concerns. It came to the same thing, in any case.

MacKinnon never walked the grounds without a rifle, his favorite being a bolt-action Husqvarna 9000 Crown Grade, chambered in 7 mm Remington Magnum. With 140-grain soft-point projectiles traveling 3,092 feet per second and striking with 2,971 foot-pounds of energy, the rifle could easily drop most four-footed prey—and would make short, bloody work of a two-legged target.

Not that MacKinnon planned to kill the trespasser outright. He hoped to grill the prowler personally, then deliver him to Laird Macauley for interrogation, but there was a possibility of armed resistance.

In which case, he would not hesitate.

The intruder was stealthy, no question about it, but Mac-

Kinnon had faith in his decades of training and natural skill. He rarely came back empty-handed from a hunt, and never when the prey was human.

This should be another easy score.

SOFT PROBES TOOK TIME. Bolan had told Beacher to check along the road from Foyers every hour or so, and keep it casual. If he was clear, he'd flag her down. If not, she'd wait another hour, then return. And so on until noon, when he'd instructed her to call a cutout number in the States, identify herself and tell whoever answered that she'd lost contact with him.

And here he was, eleven minutes in, and someone was already stalking him.

He wondered if it was the ghillie Beacher had described, Ewan MacKinnon, or some other member of Macauley's staff. The only difference would be degrees of skill and knowledge of the ground that gave the home team an advantage. Some of that was offset by the satellite surveillance photos Bolan had reviewed, but neither they nor topographic maps would give the feel of years spent on the ground, learning each wrinkle in the soil, its feel and smell.

Disappointed that an enemy had found his trail so quickly, Bolan changed his plans. Instead of making for the house, he veered off to the west through woodlands, in the general direction of Loch Ness, leading the hunter toward a place where he could choose the killing ground.

Bolan likely could not have said exactly what alerted him to being followed. Had it been a muted sound? A fleeting shadow glimpsed in peripheral vision? A sixth sense for danger, honed on battlefields around the world? Perhaps some combination of them all?

He didn't know, and at the moment didn't care. The fact of being hunted was what mattered, and the action he had to take to neutralize the threat.

In that regard, it mattered whether he was facing one man or a crew. So far, Bolan had only sensed one tracker, but a two-way radio or cell phone could be used to summon rein-forcements from the big house in a heartbeat. If that happened, if he was outnumbered and outgunned, then it became a very different scenario.

Bolan had played both games and walked away victori-ous, but at the moment—in broad daylight, on hostile ground, armed as he was—he would prefer a round of one-on-one to facing down an army.

So he would play it that way, until proved wrong, look for a place to spring a trap and turn Macauley's hunter into Bolan's prey. If he could pull it off without firing a shot, so much the better. Come what may, there would be only one survivor.

And it had to be the Executioner.

A FEW MINUTES LATER Bolan wound up going high, climbing a Scots pine and securing a perch some fifteen feet above the forest floor, screened from below by hanging boughs and needles. Not the perfect hideout, granted. Expert eyes could pick him out if they were searching overhead, but Bolan had walked past the tree, then doubled back to scale the west side of its trunk, away from the direction followed by his enemy.

Better than nothing.

Bolan waited, with the numbers running in his head, aware that if the adversary tracking him had called for help, he'd only made his situation worse by setting up an ambush. With a strike team on his trail, the wiser thing to do would be to evacuate while he still had time, before they boxed him in and sprayed his perch with automatic fire.

Too late.

The tracker was approaching, taking his time, doing it right, but still a human presence in the forest that could not be masked entirely if he chose to move at all. A stationary watcher always had the edge over a moving target, even when that target was an expert versed in the terrain. The watcher didn't need to move or make a sound, aside from breathing, while the object of his scrutiny had to advance, however slowly, cautiously, into the killing zone.

His first glimpse of the hunter was a rifle's barrel, followed by the arms supporting it and then the total man. The hunter was a husky six-footer, dressed in a camo jacket and a pair of faded blue jeans over well-worn boots. His gray hair had begun to thin around the crown, above a craggy, weathered face.

The rifle had no telescopic sight, which made it easier to aim in an emergency, but its bolt-action would delay a second shot, however briefly, if the first one missed. Bolan had no way to determine caliber from where he crouched above the rifleman, but hunters in the Highlands would be armed for red deer—Britain's largest mammal—and whichever gun Macauley's ghillie chose for that job would be powerful enough to drop a man.

Bolan drew the KA-BAR from its leather sheath, choosing the knife over his pistol in a bid to minimize the noise of what had to happen next. One shot would be enough to rouse Macauley's other men, however many there might be, but it would take a second shot—perhaps even a third—for them to pinpoint where the sounds came from. Add natural reaction time to random searching of a spread that covered several hundred acres, and he should have ample time to slip away.

If he survived that long.

The ghillie—*MacKinnon*—was almost below him, slowing his cautious pace as if he could smell danger in the air. Was that improbable? Why should Bolan be the only one endowed with warning senses in a life-or-death encounter?

Just a few more yards to go. But if he stopped or veered away, the ambush would be ruined. Worse, if he looked up into the tree…

But he came on, pausing where Bolan had deliberately scuffed the soil in passing, as if accidentally. Hardly the perfect bait, but if it held MacKinnon for a moment it was good enough.

Bolan pushed off and fell through space, rustling past pine boughs as he plummeted toward impact. Fifteen feet below, the ghillie heard him coming, spun and tried to raise his weapon, but there wasn't time to find a moving target. Bolan's right heel struck MacKinnon squarely in the face, his left impacting on the tracker's clavicle and snapping it, leaving MacKinnon's right arm useless as he fell.

It didn't stop his index finger from contracting on the rifle's trigger, though. A single shot rang out and echoed through the forest, sounding the alarm for Macauley and his men.

Before the ghillie could reverse his grip and work the rifle's bolt with his left hand, Bolan was kneeling over him and lunging with the KA-BAR, burying its clip-point blade between MacKinnon's ribs. The fallen man went stiff and shivered, as the knife's point found his heart. Bolan's free hand clamped down across his mouth, stifling a cry of pain and hanging on until the thrashing ceased at last.

So much for scoping out Macauley's property and finding out what he was up to with the *DeepScan* on Loch Ness. The probe had failed. Bolan would have to find another way inside his adversary's mind.

But first, he had to get the hell away from there.

Wiping the KA-BAR's crimson blade on camo cloth, he sheathed it and began the long jog back to where he cut a passage in the fence, checking his watch along the way to see how long he would be waiting for Beacher.

13

Alastair Macauley stood over the body of his longtime aide, chief of security and trusted friend. He felt a welling of emotion as he viewed the corpse: wool shirt and camouflage stalking jacket drenched with blood, pale face upturned, eyes blank and open to the dappled sunlight.

"Stabbed once in the pump," Graham Wallace said, with a measure of detachment that Macauley found insulting. "Looks like he took a stompin', too."

Macauley swallowed bile and anger, and said, "I wouldn't have believed he could be taken by surprise. Not in these woods."

"It took this long to find him with the acreage we had to cover," Wallace said. Then, as an afterthought, he added, "Sorry 'bout your loss, sir."

"And the men who did it? What of them?" Macauley asked.

"One man, as far as we can tell," Fergus Gibson said, standing at the laird's left elbow. "Any more, and he'd show marks from further beating."

"One man," Macauley said, insult heaped on injury.

"I ain't a woodsman," Wallace said, "but the way it looks to me, this fella climbed the tree and waited for your man to come along below him. Then he jumped down, like and finished it."

"It was his gunshot, then," Macauley said.

"Yes, sir," Wallace replied. "Rifle's been fired, but with a bolt-action he never got another."

"And no evidence that Ewan wounded the intruder?" Macauley asked.

"No blood anywheres around, 'cept his," Wallace confirmed.

"And the escape?"

"We found a hole cut in the fence," Gibson explained. "Along the south edge of the property, before it slopes down to the loch. The cuts are fresh. He used wire ties to close the flap."

"So, either Ewan found that," Macauley said, "or he met the prowler during his routine patrol."

"Whichever, sir, the creeper got the best of him," Gibson said.

"Like your own two men," Macauley said. The sudden color that he saw in Gibson's face was gratifying.

"Yes, sir. If it was the same man did both jobs, and all."

"You doubt it?" Macauley asked. "Are you saying that we have two different enemies at large in the vicinity?"

"I'm sayin' someone's pinned a target on us," Gibson answered, "but I cannot say how many are involved."

"Some kind of a conspiracy," Macauley said.

"Some kind. Yes, sir."

"And its object?" When Gibson merely blinked at him, he said, "I mean, its purpose?"

"Could be one thing or another," Gibson said evasively. "Maybe somebody doesn't like you helpin' out the TIF."

"And who would know that?" Macauley asked. "Have you broadcast our association, Mr. Gibson?"

"Me? No, sir. You need have no fear on that score."

"Well, then?"

"It could be somethin' personal to you, sir. Somethin' with your neighbors, like."

"Ridiculous! My neighbors hold me in the very highest of esteem," Macauley said. And yet, a portion of his brain was sifting names, in search of covert enemies. "What else?"

"The old kraut," Wallace interjected. "Let's not be forgettin' him, eh? A plain ol' Nazi, isn't he? I could name all kinds of folk who'd like to get their hands on him—or plug him, if they'd rather not be bothered with a trial, and all."

"What are you saying?" Macauley asked. "The Israelis? After all this time?"

Wallace responded with a lazy shrug. "I'm only sayin' it's a possibility, your lordship. If the Jews knew where to find him, or the lefty radicals from Germany, maybe…who knows?"

"We can be sure it's not the police," Gibson said, cutting off any further speculation from his second in command. "They might enjoy doin' a creep around your property, but knifin' people's not their style."

"On that," Macauley said, "we can agree."

"Unless they was the cloak-and-dagger types," Wallace said. "MI-5 and all, ya know?"

"I need to think about this," Macauley said. "And we still have preparations for the salvage operation. First, though, Ewan needs a proper burial."

"You don't mean callin' someone in?" Wallace asked.

"Don't be stupid," the laird growled. "I have all the equipment necessary, and he's already at home. Pick two or three of your best men to get it done."

WAITING WAS the worst of it, but long experience had trained Bolan to quell impatience, agitation, anger, all forms of anxiety and apprehension. While he was aware of passing time—and likely could have told Beacher what time it was without checking his watch, within two minutes either way—his face and attitude betrayed no urge to stir.

They had been parked and sitting in a scenic turnout for the past half hour, taking turns with Beacher's Bushnell glasses as they watched Macauley's wrought-iron gate, fully a quarter mile away. Bolan believed they were outside the range of any probable surveillance from the laird's estate, but close enough to pick up any vehicle that might depart from it. For props, they had two open maps, a makeshift lunch and sunglasses that would have done a tourist couple proud.

The only risk, in Bolan's mind, involved the Camry. Someone on Macauley's staff had seen it pass the gate the previous night and had decided it deserved a closer look. The men dispatched to stop them hadn't made it home, hadn't reported any further details on the car, its license number, or its passengers. Toyotas were a staple of the UK rental market, common on the roads. Easy to overlook.

They should be fine—unless they weren't. In which case, Bolan's Plan B sat behind the driver's seat in duffel bags, already locked and loaded.

"Still no police," Beacher observed. "That's good, at least."

"Macauley won't invite them back," Bolan said. "The last thing he wants is to explain another corpse right now."

"You think he'll just dispose of it himself?"

"Yes," Bolan replied. "He's got the land and an incinerator on the property. No sweat."

Beacher was peering through the glasses as they talked, when she said, "Here comes someone."

Bolan looked downrange and saw a gray sedan emerging from Macauley's gate. "Looks like another Benz," he said. "The laird likes German cars."

"To match some of his friends, apparently," Beacher observed. "We have a driver by himself, and…yes. It's Graham Wallace. Turning this way."

"Maps up," Bolan said, and they concealed their faces, leaning into each other like an average tourist couple plotting routes for a day trip, or maybe trying to determine where they'd gone wrong earlier. Moments later, when the Benz swept past, its driver barely glanced at them.

Sloppy.

Bolan gave Wallace time enough to pull away, then revved the Camry's engine, cranked it through a sharp K-turn while Beacher watched the road and set off in the TIF guerrilla's wake.

He led them back through Foyers without stopping in the village, to the B852 southbound. They followed at a cautious distance, speeding up to keep the Benz in sight on dips and winding curves, then falling back on straightaways so Wallace wouldn't pay them any mind. Arriving at the intersection with the B862, Wallace turned right and started back toward Fort Augustus.

"If he stops there, we can take him," Bolan said.

"You hope."

"It's not a problem."

"And if he keeps going? What if Gibson sent him to Fort William, then, or somewhere else?"

"I'll stop him on the way," Bolan assured her. "Either way, he's ours."

WALLACE HAD BEEN relieved when Gibson asked him to drive down and have a look around the town for anyone suspicious. How in hell he was supposed to spot a ringer? With the tourists passing through, hired cars and coaches everywhere, it was anybody's guess. But getting out from under Macauley's beady eyes was worth the drive, all by itself.

Wallace was sick and tired of kissing up to the old man, not that his view had been requested on the subject. Since they had found what they were looking for, sunk in the loch, he guessed they would be bound to Mr. High-and-Mighty Laird Macauley until the cows came home.

Or could they find a way to cut him out of it?

Wallace drove to the tourist car park, by the information kiosk and the BP station, parked and left Macauley's car, remembering to lock it with the button on the key fob. Thirty paces to his left, a mob of Japanese tourists were just unloading from a Highland Heritage coach. Two others were parked beside it from Timberbrush Tours and Highland Explorer. The clash of foreign languages bemused Wallace and made him think again of crazy Jurgen Dengler in his motorized wheelchair.

Except the old man wasn't crazy, after all.

They'd found the object that he claimed was waiting for them in the loch. Next, all they had to do was find a way to make it pay off for the Tartan Independence Front.

And Wallace wasn't looking forward to that aspect of the plan at all.

He passed along the sidewalk toward the swing bridge, rubbing shoulders with the tourists, trying not to scowl at all their jostling and jabbering. Bloody rude they were, he thought, the lot of them, acting as if they owned the place. But if they ever ceased their trips to look for Nessie, he supposed that Fort Augustus would dry up and blow away like some old mining camp from the American Wild West.

It galled him, knowing that his homeland was dependent for a great part of its income on the whims of foreigners—and all the more so when he thought about a great chunk of the profits being funneled off to England. Most of the Nessie models in the shop windows he passed were made in China, all that money gone for good behind the Bamboo Curtain to a bunch of Communists and coolies.

Could they change that, if the TIF succeeded in its bid for Scottish independence from the Crown? Wallace was hopeful, even though he didn't have a clear idea of how such changes were accomplished, or the pinch that Scots would feel during the process. Still, the Cubans had been through it, the Vietnamese, and other countries all around the world. They'd thrown off foreign dominance and still survived—thriving, most of them, with new leadership and new ideas, in his opinion.

Suspicious strangers, Wallace thought. He hadn't seen a one so far, though damn near everyone he passed was strange in one way or another. Stop a hundred people on the street in Fort Augustus, and he'd be surprised if five of them were locals.

To hell with it.

He was ready for some food, a pint or two to wash it down,

and then he could go back to the manor with a clean report. Who'd know the difference, anyhow?

He stopped outside the Bothy Restaurant and Bar, examining its menu posted on the wall. It all smelled good from where he stood—but what was that, a whiff of perfume to his left?

Wallace inhaled, smiled, was about to turn and see if he had company, when something nudged him in the ribs.

"It's a Beretta with a silencer," a male voice to his right informed him. "You can die or take a walk. Time to decide."

INSTEAD OF WALKING Wallace back through town to the car park, Bolan and Beacher escorted him along the canal's southern bank, past small stores and a newspaper shop that served as the local post office. Where the buildings thinned out, they took him aside for a frisk, Bolan relieving the Scotsman of a Browning Hi-Power pistol.

"What now?" Wallace asked.

"We go for a stroll," Bolan told him.

"You're not the police," Wallace said, frowning.

"Keep that in mind," Beacher advised him. "And your dear departed, too."

Wallace went pale at that and offered no resistance as they led him back the way they'd come, to reach the nearest foot bridge spanning the canal. Their footsteps echoed as they crossed dark water, not a boat in sight waiting for passage through the locks.

On the north side they turned right, moved past more shops and a grocery store, then turned toward the stone bridge spanning the River Oich. Across it, Bolan stopped short of the final bustling shops and car park, steering Wallace to his left. A sign directed them along a narrow gravel path to see Rare Breeds.

"In there," Bolan directed him.

Momentarily, they reached a small freestanding structure, like a ticket kiosk, which was padlocked from the outside. By the door, a drop box urged them to observe the honor system for admission fees.

Bolan stuffed a ten-pound note into the slot and told his hostage, "Go ahead." Wallace complied.

The Rare Breeds Park was larger than Bolan expected, not a petting zoo at all, but a layout spanning several acres, with separate fenced enclosures for various breeds of sheep, goats, pheasants, ducks, geese, chickens and potbellied pigs, along with Highland cattle and red deer. One of the goats sported three horns and didn't seem to mind.

The footpath they were following skirted an area roughly twice the size of a football field, with pens on both sides as they walked. As far as Bolan could tell, they were the park's only customers. He marched Wallace to the point farthest from where they had entered, beside a cluster of maintenance sheds, and announced, "Here we are."

"And where's 'here,' then?" Wallace asked, regaining a bit of bravado.

"The place where you choose if you want to survive."

"It's like that, is it?"

"In a nutshell," Bolan said.

"So, you want me to spill my guts, and you're not even coppers?"

"Three questions," Bolan told him, "and no one's expecting you to testify in court."

"I'll listen, but I promise nothin'."

Bolan let him see the 93-R with its attached sound suppressor and asked, "What's Macauley looking for, with the *DeepScan*?"

"You're onto that, eh? Well, you can go feck —"

The Parabellum slug ripped into Wallace's leg below his left knee and dropped him, with a cry of pain that echoed through the park. Bolan stepped forward and planted his right foot against the gunman's throat.

"You might have a limp, now. Want to try a wheelchair like your buddy Dengler?"

"Jaysus, man! If you know him, you've got it all worked out!"

Frowning, Bolan commanded, "So confirm it for me, then."

"The feckin' U-boat!" Wallace answered, nearly sobbing. "Somethin' the old Kraut dreamed up with his Jerry pals a hundred years ago."

"A German submarine?" Beacher demanded, clearly skeptical. "In Loch Ness?"

"Och, it's open to the sea," Wallace replied. "I need a medic now."

"We're not done," Bolan told him. "What was the U-boat supposed to do? Why does Macauley want it after all this time?"

"Some of the folk up here weren't all that keen for England in the war, ya know? Hell, they had a wanker lined up for the Crown in London, was the next thing to a Nazi but he met some Yank and tossed it in for her."

"So, Axis sympathizers," Bolan said. "Why a sub? To pick somebody up?"

Wallace giggled hysterically, shaking his head. "It weren't a pickup. It were a *delivery*. Old Heinie pricks musta known they was bound to lose the war. They start unloadin' all the shite they stole from Jews and all, layin' it off with friends."

A treasure boat.

"Something went wrong," Bolan surmised.

"And how. The damn thing sunk, whoever was expectin' it took off or died, whatever, and it gets forgotten till old Jurgen comes around."

"So there's a salvage operation under way," Bolan said.

"Starting up tonight. The laird's got his own baby submarine there, in the boathouse."

Bolan glanced at Beacher. She nodded.

"A submarine?" she asked.

"Hell yes," Wallace replied. "Surprised some yokel with it, just the other night, and had to give him the deep six."

"That raps it up," Bolan said.

"So you'll get me to the medic, then?" Wallace asked, as he tried to discreetly reach inside his jacket for a hidden gun.

But Bolan was too fast and he shot the terrorist between his eyes.

"Well, he no longer needs a medic," he said to Beacher.

ANOTHER BUFFET LUNCH. Roast beef and venison, the normal offering of vegetables and salad, with free access to the bar. Whatever shortcomings their host might have, Fergus Gibson could not fault his chef.

They'd spent an hour burying the ghillie where no one was likely to find him without methane probes and a fair idea of where to start looking. While his soldiers worked on that, Gibson had sent his number two to scout for any obvious malingerers in Fort Augustus, though he didn't hope for much on that end. Wallace had been getting antsy, even snippish toward the laird, and sending him away to cool off for a while had been a bit of strategy.

Wallace was missing lunch, but Gibson and the laird were missing his sarcastic comments, which was clearly for the best. It helped the food settle, while Gibson focused on the night ahead.

He hated the submersible. It seated three inside a metal pod with barely room enough to move once everybody was aboard. After the hatches closed and were secured, air was generated by electrolysis, while a CO_2 scrubber removed gas from the air and pumped it overboard. The major drawback was reliance on a bank of batteries to run the little sub's engine, lights, breathing apparatus and everything else.

If the batteries died at great depth, so did all hands on board.

Gibson wasn't claustrophobic, but he didn't fancy suffocating at six hundred feet with two companions whom he barely knew.

Unfortunately, their intended prize had sunk beyond the reach of scuba divers, and they couldn't advertise the operation with a deep-sea diving rig that virtually guaranteed a tourist audience on shore. The little sub, with its mechanical arms, was their only means of retrieving whatever the U-boat had carried to Scotland more than sixty years earlier.

And Laird Macauley had handpicked Gibson to go along for the ride.

So be it. As the leader of the Tartan Independence Front, it was correct and proper that he prove himself before receiving a share of the spoils. Gibson refused to think about the treasure's source—whether he might find gold ripped from the mouths of murder victims, gems that had been family heirlooms, or works of art looted from museums and from private homes.

The movement needed money to support its struggle.

And where better to find treasure than a legendary dragon's lair?

14

Bolan drove southward again on the A82, retracing his earlier route from Fort Augustus to Fort William, past Loch Lochy to Loch Eil again. He took his time without deliberately dogging it. He might have made the trip in half an hour, with a lead foot, but he wasn't needed back in Fort Augustus until dusk, still five hours ahead.

And Beacher had her own chores to complete.

The Underwater Centre at Fort William billed itself as the world's leading trainer of commercial divers and handlers of remotely operated submersible vehicles. Bolan had no idea if that claim was true, but the facility was certainly impressive. In addition to diving classes and various high-tech courses, it offered accommodation for visiting divers, serviced diving equipment and booked diving vacations.

More importantly for Bolan's needs, it rented scuba gear.

After showing his Matt Cooper ID, Visa card and current master diver's certification, Bolan began collecting the gear he would need. He started with a dry suit, since the average water surface temperature at Loch Ness rarely topped a chilly fifty-four degrees that time of year. Though he didn't plan on going deep—no more than thirty feet, if all went well—hypothermia would put a fatal crimp in his plans.

Once he'd been fitted for the suit, Bolan proceeded with the other gear he needed: mask and swim fins, an underwater flashlight, a single diving cylinder with dual regulators to allow for failure underwater, a mandatory buoyancy compensator for safety's sake and ditchable weights to offset the last item. Bolan paid cash for three days' rental, left his Visa number as a hedge in case the gear wasn't returned and lugged the outfit to his Camry in the center's parking lot.

Diving had been a part of Bolan's early Special Forces training, mandatory to secure a Green Beret, although it wasn't emphasized to the degree of Navy SEAL instruction. The course he'd passed included underwater demolition, pioneered in World War II for clearing hostile beaches and refined over the years to cover "clearance" work on sunken wrecks and other obstacles, along with sabotage of surface vehicles.

Or submarines. Why not?

Along the way, he'd practiced fighting underwater—barehanded, with knives, and whatever else came to hand as a weapon—but Bolan doubted that he'd need that particular skill at Fort Augustus. His goal was to disable Macauley's private submarine, and maybe sink the *DeepScan* in the bargain. If he managed to accomplish that, no matter what might happen next, he would have stalled the laird's treasure hunt and kept a hoard of loot from falling into terrorist hands.

And if he had a chance to deal with Jurgen Dengler somewhere down the road, so much the better.

When most people thought about the Holocaust these days, they naturally focused on the death camps. Millions slaughtered in the name of "racial purity" or worked to death in service of the so-called "master race." Largely forgotten was the fact that Adolf Hitler and his inner circle were a gang of world-class racketeers who cynically embarked on wholesale looting of occupied Europe for personal profit.

Behind the cockeyed ideals of Teutonic supremacy, closet occultism and ethnic cleansing, the old-school Nazis were murderous thieves. No one could say with any certainty how much they stole between 1933 and 1945, before the "Thousand-Year Reich" collapsed in bloody chaos, but Hermann Göring's personal collection had included some two thousand

pieces of art, three hundred priceless paintings among them.
Hitler's Austrian Führermuseum was a storehouse for plunder,
while other caches were known to exist at Nazi headquarters
in Munich and at the Musée du Jeu de Paume in Paris.

Bottom line: an estimated twenty percent of all art in
Europe was stolen by Nazis, along with incalculable wealth
stripped from individual families. Sixty-six years and counting since Hitler's suicide, more than one hundred thousand art
objects were still missing.

And if Bolan had his way, not one would go to fund the
Tartan Independence Front.

WITH COOPER off in the car, Beacher walked down to Loch
Ness on her own. Out through the front door of the lodge,
where the black Lab was still on station as a greeter, then
across the parking lot and down the curving driveway to the
two-lane highway at its end. Instead of turning to the right
and hiking the half mile to Fort Augustus, she crossed there,
turned left and walked against oncoming traffic for three hundred yards.

Her destination was a turnout where a narrow loop of
blacktop left the highway, dipping to the loch's shore down
below. There was a stingy parking area, a gravel beach with
thistles sprouting at its limits and a pair of jetties used for
launching small boats on the loch. She was below road level,
the traffic hissing past above her head.

Within the next half hour or so, a car would slow, pull off
the road and dip downhill to park. Until that time, she was
content to find a boulder and sit atop it, watching anglers on
the loch and puddling ducks closer to shore. A hen passed by
with half a dozen chicks in tow, ducking their heads from time
to time, a quacking convoy dining on the smaller bounty of
Loch Ness.

The call she'd made had been a gamble. Least among the
risks involved had been rejection of the plan she'd hatched
with Cooper. A worse scenario had been her recall from the

field to face a hearing for misconduct, with potential for indictment, trial, imprisonment. If someone higher on the bureaucratic food chain had decided it should play that way, there'd be no record of her orders to proceed with Cooper in Glasgow and beyond.

But none of that had come to pass. The answer to her call had been affirmative—which might lead Beacher to the worst scenario of all. Say sudden death, for instance.

Staring northward and across the loch, she pictured Macauley in his big house, huddled with surviving members of the TIF contingent and his ancient Nazi colleague. She supposed that Dengler would be listed as a technical adviser if their grim adventure was a movie production. As it stood, however, he was just a monster who had lived beyond his time.

She heard a car slowing above her, followed by a rasp of tires on gravel as it coasted down to lochside. Beacher took her time retreating from the water's edge. The driver stepped out of his Ford and stretched a bit. She didn't recognize him, knew that it would be an unfamiliar face behind the wheel. A hurry call like hers allowed no time for sending anyone she knew from Glasgow, much less up from London.

Never mind.

She showed ID and he reciprocated. Arthur Bancroft, from Britain's National Extremism Tactical Coordination Unit—NETCU—a branch of the Association of Chief Police Officers tasked with tactical advice and guidance on suppression of what the government called "single-issue domestic extremism." That description clearly fit the TIF, but this time Bancroft was providing more than guidance, more than tactical advice.

"I normally don't make deliveries like this," he said.

"These are abnormal times," Beacher replied.

"Apparently. You've handled this equipment in the past, I take it?"

"Not a problem," she assured him.

"Right, then."

Opening the back door on the driver's side, Bancroft removed a gym bag, frowning as he passed it to Beacher. She pegged its weight somewhere in the vicinity of twenty pounds.

"If there's nothing else you need…?"

"Just you forgetting you were ever here," she said.

"My specialty," Bancroft replied. "Good luck to you."

She stood and watched the Ford roll out and back onto the highway, headed north toward Inverness. When it was gone, Beacher took one last look across the loch, then started back to the hotel.

BOLAN WAS TIRED of waiting, but he needed daylight to retreat before he launched his next move against Alastair Macauley and his cronies of the TIF. Accordingly, he'd stopped with Beacher at a scenic spot most tourists overlooked: a waterfall that plunged 140 feet into the River Foyers, running a hydro-electric plan that fed Scotland's national grid.

Beacher ignored the scenery and asked him, "Are you sure about this, then?"

"I'm sure," Bolan replied.

At the hotel, he'd shown Beacher the scuba gear, explaining how it worked, the double regulator's fail-safe mechanism, but she hadn't been appeased. With only three quarters of an hour left until he went into the water, she renewed her personal objections.

"We can rent a boat," she said. "Go past and wreck his little navy from the surface."

"Not with the equipment that we have," Bolan said. "My rifle and grenades might do some damage to the *DeepScan*, but I likely couldn't sink it. And there'd be no way of knowing if we even hit the sub, inside the boathouse."

"Can't you get some rockets, then?" she challenged him. "Something to do the job without you swimming underwater, in the dark, around Loch Ness?"

"You got the limpet mines," Bolan reminded her. He'd checked and armed them at the lodge. "And I have a light."

Which would be used discreetly, to avoid alerting any watchers on the shore.

"I just don't like this," Beacher said.

He smiled. "Look, if the monster's got you worried—"

"No, dammit! *Macauley* has me worried. And his playmates. If they're on the verge of bringing up this treasure, don't you think they'll be on guard?"

"I doubt that they'll consider anyone approaching from the loch, submerged," Bolan replied. "And if they do…"

He'd double bagged the Spectre SMG in plastic, sealed with duct tape. With its loaded magazine and sound suppressor attached, it added nine pounds to his total weight, which Bolan counted as a benefit for traveling submerged. He still had thirty feet selected as his ideal depth and planned to let the east shore of the loch guide him as he swam southward, from the outlet of the River Foyers to Macauley's dock and boathouse, something like a quarter mile below.

Easy enough. Unless an unexpected current sucked him out into the loch and took him deeper than his gear and lungs could handle. Or unless Macauley's lookouts saw him coming and decided they could risk a fusillade of shots to sink him.

And if he was eaten by a monster, who would ever know?

"What's funny?" Beacher asked him.

Hardly conscious that he had been smiling, Bolan answered, "Nothing. I enjoy the peace and quiet here, is all."

"So let's stay here," she said. "Forget about this frogman scheme and find another way to stop Macauley."

"Taking out the *DeepScan* and the sub won't stop Macauley," Bolan said. "It's just a means to slow him. I'll stop him afterward."

"You mean *we* will," she said.

"If you're still with me," Bolan countered.

"Jesus, you're a stubborn bugger," Beacher said. "All right, let's go and drop you in the loch, shall we? It's almost time."

THE CHAPEL WAS a small but solemn place, devoted to the Church of Scotland. Alastair Macauley's great-grandfather had constructed it in 1865, three-quarters of a century before the British Parliament in London recognized the Church of Scotland's full independence from the Church of England.

One more bloody insult: John Bull telling Scots how they should worship, even as he stole their land and livelihood, defiled their daughters under *Jus primae noctis,* and hanged their sons for treason if they dared resist.

It pained him that the Brits would never truly suffer for their crimes, but with the newfound wealth that waited for him in the loch, Macauley could finance a grim war of attrition that would make them pay in blood, until they squealed for mercy.

"And you're sure about the contents of the submarine?" he asked.

"*Ja, ja.* Unless your dragon of the lake has stolen it," Dengler replied. "Twelve hundred kilograms of gold, five hundred kilograms of cut diamonds, plus assorted other gems."

The gold alone, at that morning's price in London, exceeded thirty-five-and-a-half million pounds. The cache of diamonds, while smaller and subject to flexible pricing, was vastly more valuable—somewhere in the neighborhood of four *billion* pounds.

A king's ransom, and then some.

King Alastair the First?

Macauley had no such royal aspirations, but he would gladly accept nomination as his homeland's first prime minister. And if Macauley's people deemed that he should rule for life, how could he refuse them? He would be benevolent, of course. Attentive to the needs of every Scot and zealous in defending Scotland's reputation. And if the Brits wanted oil and natural gas to keep flowing from the drilling rigs in Scottish waters, they could damned well raise the ante.

With a nice percentage for the laird.

Why shouldn't a patriot benefit from his sacrifice for the good of his nation?

"I know that look," Dengler said, leering from his wheelchair. "I've seen it before. You remind me of Field Marshal Göring."

"I'm nothing like him!" Macauley snapped.

"Oh, no? Great men of great appetite, *ja?* What separates you, then?"

"If you have to ask, you wouldn't understand," Macauley said.

"Perhaps I understand enough," Dengler replied. "You hate England and use me as a weapon to punish them, eh? If you had lived during the war, you would have kissed *der Führer*'s ass and pledged allegiance to the Reich against your monarch."

Macauley felt a sudden surge of anger, barely understood what he was doing as he grasped the decorative candlestick, an ancient thing of heavy brass. Dengler was smirking at him as he turned, but the expression on his wizened face transformed itself into a mask of shock, then fear, as he picked out the weapon in Macauley's fist.

The first blow may have cracked the German's skull. He should have been dead by the fourth or fifth, but still Macauley kept on swinging. Eight, nine, ten times with the two-foot candlestick, until its base was dripping crimson and his tweed jacket was deeply stained.

He rang for Bruce then, waited for his butler to survey the scene and said, "Fetch Mr. Wallace and his lads. They need to dig another hole."

BOLAN SWAM SOUTHWARD from the headland where the River Foyers spilled into the loch, its mouth divided by a wedge-shaped island. He felt buoyant in the cloudy water, even with the submachine gun strapped across his chest and the two limpet mines trailing beside him in a fishnet bag. At thirty feet below the surface, swimming in Loch Ness was much like crawling at the bottom of a coal mine, but without the scrapes to hands and knees.

He used the flashlight sparingly, to keep track of the shore-line on his left and thus avoid veering off course. In terms of distance, Bolan knew approximately how fast he was swimming—say one mile an hour with the load he carried, and his pace of kicking with the swim fins. Call it twenty minutes for a quarter mile.

As Bolan swam, he thought about the fish inhabiting Loch Ness. The only two that posed a threat of any kind to divers were the pike, voracious ambush predators, and European eels, reported to exceed six feet in length. Both could deliver painful bites, but Bolan knew of no cases where either had attacked a diver. If they did, he had the KA-BAR lashed to his right thigh, where he could reach it easily.

If he still had an arm.

Though he was keeping track of time, Macauley's dock and boathouse almost took him by surprise. Bolan picked out the *DeepScan* first, his flashlight beam sliding along its hull, before he found the boathouse braced on pillars jutting outward from the rocky shore. As he'd expected, it was open from below, allowing any craft it housed to stay afloat.

Bolan removed the first mine from its pocket in the fishnet bag. It was a limpet charge, equipped with magnets on the back and strips of powerful adhesive for a backup, if the target vessel's hull was made of fiberglass. It was a British model, obviously, meaning that its plastic charge weighed four kilograms. Attached six feet below the waterline, it was designed to blow a yard-wide hole in any ship's unarmored hull.

Bolan took his time placing the charge, avoiding any clank of contact in case there was someone aboard. He pressed a button to arm the mine's remote-control detonator, then swam off toward the boathouse.

Entering blind through the structure's open floor was risky. A gunman on watch there, sitting in darkness, could fire through the neoprene hood of his dry suit before Bolan knew he'd been spotted. He lingered outside for a moment, therefore, with his flashlight extinguished, watching for lights from within while he listened for any stray sounds that the water might carry.

Nothing.

At last, still without surfacing, he approached Macauley's submersible. Its hull felt rough, even through Bolan's gloves. But it was definitely metal, and he placed the other limpet mine up near the nose, where he felt lights attached, and other kinds of gear that he supposed were used for salvage missions.

When the second mine was armed, he ducked out of the boathouse, used his flashlight long enough to orient himself, then began the quarter-mile return trip to the north. Beacher would be waiting for him, hopefully without a nosy local resident or constable to keep her company, but just in case, he was prepared with a diversion.

Bolan found a place to surface, slipped the small remote-control device out of a pouch that held it on his weight belt and armed it with the flick of a switch. A small red light glowed in his palm, obscured by the loch's murky water.

Would the signal reach its destination?

Only one way to find out.

He keyed the detonator, and the double blast echoed across Loch Ness an instant later. Gazing southward through his dive mask, breathing bottled air, Bolan couldn't see a fireball, since the charges both exploded underwater. There was no great waterspout to see in darkness, either, but the sound was adequate to tell him that his mission was successful.

This part of it, anyway.

He hadn't stopped Macauley yet, but that came next.

The Executioner was blitzing on.

15

The *DeepScan* had not sunk, exactly, since its mooring ropes still bound it to the dock, but it had rolled to starboard, taking water through a great wound in its hull, and settled there. It didn't take an engineer to know that if the lines were cut, the research vessel would be gone in minutes flat.

The three-man submarine, likewise, was moored inside the boathouse, but with one line at the bow. Therefore, as it had filled with water, it had settled to the stern, straining its line. Only the rounded nose was still above water, its spotlights and spindly mechanical arms making the crippled boat resemble some freak from the depths washed ashore by the tide.

"How likely is it that the blasts won't be reported?" Gibson asked.

Macauley seethed with fury, standing next to Gibson on his private dock, flanked by a pair of soldiers from the TIF. "I call the chances slim to none," he answered through clenched teeth. "We heard them well enough inside the house up there. Sound carries on the water."

"At least the boathouse wasn't damaged," Gibson said. "Whoever comes, maybe they'll only see the *DeepScan*."

"Which is bloody bad enough," Macauley answered. "But you won't win any races taking them for idiots. The water bailiff knows his job, and we'll have CID back here by morning. Mark my words."

"No problem, with the cover story," Gibson said. "We've got those threats on file, against the monster hunt. That crazy witch from Perth who cursed the *DeepScan,* and the Barrhead tree huggers. The police can chase them around."

"While we do what, pray tell? Take up collections for a new submersible? Maybe your witch can conjure up a suitable replacement?"

"I just meant—"

"Stop trying to console me, damn it! This has set us back immeasurably."

Looking abashed, Gibson replied, "They missed the speedboat, anyhow."

That much was true. The saboteurs had overlooked his Spencer Runabout, moored in the boathouse with the little submarine, attacking only vessels earmarked for the salvage job.

Which meant…

"They had to know," Macauley said.

Gibson looked confused. "What do you mean?"

"About the U-boat," Macauley said. "You and I know that it wasn't monster lovers or environmentalists who did this. Someone else knows what we're doing here."

"Don't look at me," Gibson replied. After a glance to the left and right, he leaned closer and said, "I haven't even told my men."

"But Wallace knows."

"Of course *he* knows, but Graham—"

"Where's he gotten off to, by the way? It's all of two miles down to Fort Augustus. Is he staying overnight and just forgot to call?"

"You know I sent him in to look around for strangers," Gibson said.

"And do you think they have a mob of tourists on the street, this time of night? For Christ's sake, man! They roll the bloody sidewalks up at sundown."

"I can send someone to look for him," Gibson said.

"No! I lose another car each time you send one of your people out to sniff around. We'll all soon be afoot, at this rate."

"Graham won't run out on us," Gibson protested. "We've been friends since we were kids."

"Then something's happened to him. Like the others," Macauley said.

"Jaysus," Gibson muttered. "What if it's the old kraut's buddies, then?"

"Dengler? He's dead, if you've forgotten."

"I've forgotten nothin'," Gibson said. "But what if he's been playin' us along this whole time? Usin' you to bring his goodies up for Scotland, all the while waitin' to steal 'em back again."

"And who's done this?" Macauley asked him, nodding toward the *DeepScan*. "Who killed your two men at Boleskine House, and Ewan in my own backyard? Have you seen any ancient Germans hobbling around with little Nazi banners hanging from their walkers?"

"He could afford a crop of young ones," Gibson said. "It's not like all the fascists in the world are pensioners, ya know."

"All right. Send *one* man into town, in *your* car. Look for my Mercedes first, then Wallace. Have him call if he finds anything, then come directly back."

"Yes, sir."

"With no goddamn delays," Macauley said.

He had a feeling that they might need every gun available, and soon.

SOMEONE HAD FOUND the makeshift gate cut in Macauley's fence and made an effort to repair it, using wire and solder until new chain link could be installed. Rather than waste time on the old flap, Bolan cut a new one twenty feet farther along the fence and wriggled through, then held it open for Beacher.

Their time was tight. Instead of waiting for police to come and go, Bolan had opted for a follow-up within the hour, rushing through a change from his dry suit and diving gear to dark clothes for the final penetration of Macauley's property. Beacher was carrying the Spectre SMG, bone-dry when Bolan took it from its plastic wrap after his swim, with extra magazines weighting her pockets. He had the Steyr AUG and his Beretta, with the last of his L-109 grenades clipped to his belt.

The soldier had gambled that the action on Macauley's private dock would have most of the men assigned to keep the grounds secure. Bolan had never managed to secure a head count for the home team, but his best guess made it ten to twelve men overall. Importing more might have sparked gossip in the local pubs and over backyard fences, ultimately getting back to the police.

Say twelve, then, minus three. If there were fewer hardmen on the property, so much the better. And if he'd underestimated? Then he would simply have to hit them that much harder in the time available.

The grounds were dark, the footing tricky, but a blaze of lights from the mansion kept him and Beacher on course. Bolan's priority, job one, was cutting off his enemy's retreat. He didn't want them hopping into cars and racing off to Inverness or Timbuktu before he had a chance to deal with them.

No exit from the killing ground this time.

His list of targets was a relatively short one: Alastair Macauley, Fergus Gibson, Jurgen Dengler. Anyone in their employ who stood against him was fair game, but those were the top three. Eliminate them, and the fishing expedition at Loch Ness was done—at least until word got around and someone from the government showed up to claim the prize.

Three hundred yards and closing to the big house, still no guards in sight. Bolan was angling off toward the four-car garage, two sedans parked out in front of it, when a man emerged from the house and angled toward the nearest of the cars. Keys jangled in his hand as he approached, then taillights winked on a Honda Accord as he opened the locks remotely.

No one leaves.

Bolan shifted the Steyr to his left hand, drawing the silenced Beretta with his right. He sprinted toward the stranger in the driveway, footsteps muffled on thick grass but audible.

The stranger turned with a pinched expression on his face, his free hand drifting underneath his windbreaker.

Bolan squeezed off a double-tap from thirty feet and put him down, the dead man's legs collapsing under him. Beacher closed the gap as Bolan reached the Honda, slowing, stepping around the corpse as he moved on to the garage.

Step one: deny the enemy mobility.

Bolan opened a side door to the long garage and stepped inside.

FERGUS GIBSON TRIED Graham Wallace's cell phone again, heard it ring four times, then switch over to voice mail. He snapped his phone shut, cutting off the message that he knew by heart.

"I'm busy at the moment. If you wanna leave a number—"

"Stupid bastard!" Gibson muttered, feeling guilty even as he said it. Wallace wouldn't simply take off in Macauley's Benz and leave them hanging, would he? After all that they'd been through together since they were a pair of snot-nosed kids running the streets. Something had to have happened, but—

The floor shuddered beneath him, as a hellacious bang rattled the walls and windows. Wallace heard glass break somewhere in the mansion, couldn't place it and didn't frankly give a damn. He had to find out what was happening, before—

Another blast, then, louder than the first, as if a string of giant firecrackers was going off outside. Recognizing the general direction from which the blasts had come from, he rushed through the house to find a window facing on the driveway and garage. When Wallace did find one, it was shattered, and he saw the reason why.

The two cars Gibson and his men had driven to Macauley's place when they began the *DeepScan* operation were in flames. A body lay beside one of them, likely Dickie Cameron, whom he had told to look for Wallace down in Fort Augustus. Dead, with his trousers burning, not a twitch to show he felt it. And beyond the blasted cars, Macauley's long garage was blazing like a bonfire, fueled by gasoline from the laird's Mercedes-Benz collection. What was left of it, that was.

Wallace quickly realized that aside from the dead ghillie's little Honda motorcycle, he and his crew were officially on foot.

He glimpsed a shadow, someone running on the far side of the leaping flames—or was it *two* people? Wallace couldn't be sure. For all he knew, an army could be circling the mansion as he stood there, gaping at the damage they'd already done.

It was time to move.

Wallace drew his pistol, a Heckler & Koch P2000, and held it ready against any threat as he went looking for Macauley. The old man had snapped with Dengler, but that was one grave-digging Wallace had been pleased to supervise. The animated mummy had repulsed him personally, and the thought of handing off one-quarter of the treasure to a Nazi prick was galling. Never mind where all that loot had come from in the first place. It was finders keepers, and he thought an old man on his last legs—or without them, in the German's case—should have been happy with the table scraps.

No time to think about that, though, as he heard the rattle of gunfire from outside the manor house. Nine men remaining to him on the property—no, eight, with Cameron down—and Gibson started shouting for them, calling them from every nook and cranny in the mansion.

Some, he knew, were already outside, beyond his reach unless he stepped into the shooting gallery. How many might be dead or dying at that very moment he could not surmise. But every man that he could gather, every hand that he could arm, would be an asset.

Macauley kept a stash of weapons hidden in his trophy room, behind a cabinet displaying his approved and licensed guns. Tucked out of sight were something like a dozen automatic rifles and as many handguns, laid by with emergencies in mind, and ample ammunition for a standoff with the police, if it came to that.

But these weren't coppers raiding the grounds on this night. The men and women with badges didn't creep around and blow up cars—at least, not before announcing themselves. So it was someone else, not planning to arrest Macauley or his visitors.

It was a killing situation.

Starting this second.

BEACHER SQUEEZED OFF a short burst from the submachine gun Cooper had loaned her. She heard spent casings tinkle on the driveway's pavement but saw her target drop and roll to cover at the southeast corner of the house. A miss and three or four rounds wasted, then.

When Cooper had started blowing up the cars outside Macauley's house, it brought four gunmen rushing to investigate the racket. Beacher had expected more and was relieved by the small turnout at a glance, until the shooting started. After that, it was a scramble to survive and drop the only kind of targets that really mattered.

The kind that shot back.

The four shooters she'd seen so far were not familiar to her. TIF, most likely, but no sign of Gibson or the laird. And if the bosses were inside, it stood to reason that they had to have other gunmen with them, for security. At least one bodyguard apiece, more likely two or three. She and Cooper would never know, unless they managed to eliminate the first four without getting tagged themselves.

Beacher knew there was no such thing as "just a flesh wound," when it came to gunfire. Hollywood writers portrayed action heroes leaping around like Olympic gymnasts with slugs in their shoulders, but that was a ripe crock of shite, she thought. Even a simple dislocation of the shoulder could be crippling; never mind a bullet ripping through the muscles, bones and tendons there.

She moved to keep a burning car between herself and the gunman her last shots had missed. Flames wouldn't stop bullets, but they could hide her while spoiling her adversary's night vision, hopefully giving Beacher a small edge. Meanwhile, the heat was baking her face, while the smell of burned flesh on the man Cooper had shot turned her stomach.

Buck up, she silently chastised herself, and get it done.

Beacher had volunteered for this, against her better judgment, and she obviously couldn't change her mind this late in the game. The stakes were nothing less than personal survival.

The gunman showed himself again, maybe believing she'd retreated or pushed on to breach the house. Whatever he was thinking, cautious as he was, he gave Beacher a shot.

She took it without hesitation. Three rounds from a range of forty feet, and she saw two of them strike home. Twin puffs of crimson burst from the target's upper chest before he toppled over backward in a boneless sprawl.

Two down, that she was sure of, and the rattle of Cooper's assault rifle told her that he'd found another target. One more down, she guessed, from having seen the big American work, but had more crept out of Macauley's house in the meantime? Were they circling around to come at her from some new direction, out of the darkness while her eyes were dazzled by firelight?

"Ready?"

The question came from Beacher's left, Cooper suddenly beside her, nearly making her jump. She scanned the driveway and the grounds that she could see for other living threats, then nodded.

"When you are," she said.

"This way."

They were off and running, then, to find the laird and Gibson, with however many men they still had left. Hopefully they'd succeed before police arrived and Beacher had to tell the story she'd been working on in private, since she first closed ranks with Cooper.

Would anyone believe it?

Would she even live to try it on for size?

BLITZING THE MOTOR POOL had only been part one of Bolan's battle plan. Leaving his enemies without a means to flee, except on foot, was only beneficial if he found the targets he was seeking.

Alastair Macauley. Fergus Gibson. Jurgen Dengler.

Taking out the Nazi fugitive would be a bonus, but it wasn't central to the job at hand. In realistic terms, he wouldn't live much longer, and he'd never mount another expedition to retrieve the stolen loot of Europe from Loch Ness. That ship had sailed—or, rather, sunk—before Dengler could salvage any remnant of his Fourth Reich fantasy.

The Tartan Independence Front, however, still remained a clear and present danger. Bolan had an opportunity to nail its founder and its financier in one sweep, if he didn't get distracted by their pawns and let the big fish slip away.

A rifleman was waiting for them as they neared the house, jogging through smoke and dappled firelight toward a door that likely opened on the kitchen or a service area. The watchman missed his first shot, being hasty, and the bullet cracked concrete a foot or so to Bolan's left. It was warning enough to make him duck and dodge, while Beacher took her own evasive steps behind him.

Muzzle-flashes marked the next burst, winking from what Bolan took to be a kitchen window. Bullets whispered past him in the smoky night, as he hit a shoulder roll and scrabbled toward the cover of a tree that loomed between the house and what was left of the garage. Once there, he took stock of the situation, judging angles and his distance from the enemy.

Not easy, but he thought it might be possible.

Beacher had reached the tree a heartbeat after Bolan, cursing at a near miss from the sniper. Bolan verified that she was still uninjured, while he palmed his final frag grenade and pulled its pin.

She caught the move and said, "From here?"

"It's worth a try," he told her. "Cover me, on three."

She nodded, and he started counting. "One…two…"

And on *three* she ducked around the far side of the tree trunk, blazing with the Spectre M-4 toward the window where their adversary stood. A storm of Parabellum slugs gave Bolan time to step out, make his pitch and duck back under cover as the lethal egg flew toward its mark.

Four seconds later, smoke and shattered masonry spewed from the kitchen window, smothering a human squeal. Bolan was off and running for the door at once, with Beacher close behind him, both their weapons covering the window sniper's nest. No further challenge from that quarter, as Bolan gave the door a flying kick and lunged across the threshold.

Shrapnel hadn't killed the shooter outright, but he was a bloody mess when Bolan found him, stitched from chin to shins and bleeding from at least a hundred wounds. Even in that extremity, the Scotsman tried to reach the automatic rifle that had fallen from his hands as he went down.

He never made it.

Bolan put a single round between the sniper's glassy eyes and left him trembling in his death throes, moving on to find Macauley, Gibson and Dengler in the rambling house. They had to be somewhere close at hand, since there was no way for them to escape.

Or was there?

Had he missed something?

"What is it?" Beacher asked him, frowning at the look on Bolan's face.

"Nothing," he said. "Let's get it done."

16

Liam Abercrombie was late. He'd been chasing a couple of young drunks from Dores who were going wild on Jet Skis, and it had taken him some time to run them down. Then, in the midst of writing their citations, came the phone call from the constable in Fort Augustus, claiming someone had reported explosions in the neighborhood of Alastair Macauley's dock.

Abercrombie had been looking forward to his supper, with a pint or two, but it seemed he had another job to handle. As he motored southward on the loch, he thought about the sort of things that might produce such a report.

Some kind of accident aboard the *DeepScan*, possibly, resulting in explosion of its fuel. Or something in the boathouse, where Macauley kept a speedboat and the weird little submersible he'd bought to search the bottom of the loch. The sub ran on electric power, but the speedboat burned gasoline, and there were likely spare drums waiting to refill its tanks.

The worst scenario would be if he discovered that Macauley had been dropping charges in the loch, as part of his bizarre attempt to find the beastie. That would land the old man in hot water, laird or not, and fines might not be good enough to cover it.

That said, arresting Macauley would require conclusive evidence, not idle speculation or the say-so of disgruntled neighbors. Abercrombie knew that if he moved against the laird, he'd have to make it stick.

Or else he'd be out of a job.

As he approached Macauley's dock and boathouse, Abercrombie saw the *DeepScan* listing mightily to starboard, with its wheelhouse almost horizontal. Nothing but its mooring lines had kept the research boat from going down. The water bailiff swept his spotlight's beam along the vessel's length and found no damage visible, but when he shifted to the boathouse there were several fresh-looking holes along the waterline.

Before he had the chance to take a closer look, he was distracted by a popping sound like fireworks overhead. Frowning, the bailiff craned his neck to get a long view of Macauley's mansion on the hilltop.

What in hell was going on? Some kind of celebration?

No.

A fair outdoorsman in his own right, Abercrombie recognized the fireworks as reports from several different weapons. Suddenly, as he stood listening, there came the rattle of an automatic firearm high above him.

Christ! Machine guns?

And the damage to the *DeepScan* wouldn't be an accident. Somehow, for reasons Abercrombie could not fathom, Macauley's great house on the hill had come under attack. The fight was in full swing, and there was nothing that an unarmed water bailiff could do to stop it.

Nothing but ringing up the police, if they hadn't heard the news already. One young constable on duty for the evening, and what could *he* do, if it came to that? Nothing, most likely, but alert his headquarters in Inverness.

And what could they do in a hurry, he wondered, sitting sixty-three miles away to the north? Even at top speed on the narrow lochside roads, they'd need the best part of an hour to arrive. How many people would be dead or maimed by then?

How many were already dead?

Heartsick and feeling helpless, Abercrombie made the call and settled down to wait.

BOLAN CLEARED the kitchen, moving onward to a formal dining room. Places had been set for two—a puzzler; why not three, at least?—but nothing had been served.

The Executioner had spoiled Macauley's appetite.

There would be no last supper for the laird.

Bolan took one side of the table, and Beacher the other, as they cleared the dining room. Somewhere in front of them, above them, or around them in adjacent rooms, there had to be men with guns—Macauley, certainly; his crony Gibson and the aged fascist, Dengler. Add in bodyguards, likely a team of TIF guerrillas, ready to defend their leader and his moneymen.

But where were they?

It would take time to search a house so large, and they could wind up playing hide-and-seek like characters in some demented bedroom farce until police rolled up with sirens whooping.

Unacceptable.

A wise exterminator didn't waste time chasing rats around inside a maze. He smoked them out.

But where to start?

Right here.

The dining room was heated by a large stone fireplace set into the north wall. Someone on Macauley's staff had laid a fire and lit it, but had not returned to tend it. It was guttering when Bolan dragged the fireplace screen aside and used a poker to revive the flames.

"What are you doing?" Beacher asked, from the doorway to another room.

"Housewarming," Bolan answered, as the flames leaped higher, burning bright.

He took the poker with him to the dining table, yanked its tablecloth free with a crash and clatter of china, and wound it around the poker's pronged tip to make a crude torch. Returning to the fireplace, Bolan lit it and began to move around the large room, setting fire to drapes and tapestries.

In seconds, flames were climbing up the polished wooden walls and he was moving toward Beacher with blazing torch in hand, its heat strong on his face. She stepped aside to let him pass, the shrinking tablecloth trailing sparks on the carpet.

"You'll roast us all at this rate," she advised him.

"Rats first," Bolan told her. "When they get a whiff of smoke, they'll start to run."

"And if they don't?" she asked.

"Their choice," Bolan replied. "Come out and play, or sit and burn."

He didn't check the look she gave him, had no time to think about her sensibilities. Their time was short, and Bolan didn't plan to leave his enemies alive.

Degüello, right.

No quarter asked or offered, to the bloody end.

"THAT'S SMOKE," Macauley said. "Do you smell it?"

Gibson sniffed the air, smelled something, but he wasn't sure. "I couldn't say," he answered finally.

"It's definitely smoke," Macauley said. "There's something badly wrong."

"Don't panic, eh?" Gibson advised him. "We're good here."

Here being Macauley's study on the second floor, behind a stout door bolted shut. Gibson was sitting on a corner of Macauley's massive teakwood desk, with an M-4 carbine propped across his knee. A shorter version of the M-16 assault rifle, it had the same firepower as its parent weapon but weighed two pounds less with a loaded 30-round magazine.

Macauley had initially resisted picking out a weapon for himself, but finally chose a Benelli M-4 Super 90 shotgun from the hidden rack, loaded with double-00 buckshot rounds. It lay across the desk, its muzzle pointed in the general direction of the bolted door, while Macauley sat in his high-backed throne of a chair with his hands in his lap.

Sniffing the air like a hound on the hunt, mustache bristling, the laird said again, "There's no question. That's smoke."

Before Gibson could answer, one of his men standing by said, "I smell it too, Fergus."

"All right, so you smell it," he said. "That doesn't mean—"

A hammering against the study door cut short his answer. Yet another of his men, this one outside, clamored, "The house is burnin'! Ever'body out!"

Macauley bolted to his feet, saying, "I knew it!" He was halfway to the door before remembering his weapon, doubled back and grabbed the shotgun from his desk. He glared at Gibson and demanded, "Are you coming?"

"Coming where, exactly?" Gibson asked.

"To get the hell away from here," Macauley said.

"You might've noticed that the cars are blown to shite," Gibson replied. "Unless you want to hike out past whoever's shooting up the place, we need to think this through."

"I've thought it through," Macauley said. "And we're not hiking anywhere."

"What, then?"

"The speedboat," Macauley said. "We can be away before these bastards know it."

Gibson followed, with his two men trailing, picking up the third outside. It meant going downstairs, but he could definitely smell the smoke by this point and didn't feel like being roasted if there was another option.

Once he'd got it in his head to move, Macauley wasted no time charging down the stairs and back along a corridor that ran the full width of the house. When they were almost to the exit, someone shouted out Macauley's name behind them, a male voice that Gibson didn't recognize. He turned to see two figures—*Christ, was one of them a woman?*—at the far end of the hallway, following.

"Stay here and finish 'em," he told two of his soldiers, solid Dillon Bryce and Georgie Souter. "Catch up when you're done." Not bothering to see if they were happy with the order, as he turned and ran after Macauley, out into the night.

The chairlift was too slow. They took the stairs, moving

as fast as possible without risking a headlong tumble to the dock and water below. Gibson saw an unexpected boat drawn up beside the *DeepScan,* someone standing in it, watching them descend. He didn't recognize the local water bailiff, but a glimpse of the man's badge was all he needed.

Firing from the hip, Gibson put half a dozen rounds into the stranger, dumped him over backward from his boat and down into the loch.

THE REAR-GUARD SHOOTERS did their best, which wasn't much. They fired all right, but high and wide in haste, with shaky hands. Their slugs chewed up Macauley's paneled walls and ceiling, while Bolan and Beacher fired back on point and put them down.

Which left three others out the door and in the wind.

"I recognized Macauley," Beacher said. "And Gibson with him, plus some character I've never seen before."

"Their cover," Bolan said, already moving toward the door that his vanished prey had left wide open on the night. It caused a draft and drew smoke from the burning house along behind them as they ran.

A moment's cautious hesitation on the threshold, then Bolan was out and clear, sweeping the open ground before him with the Steyr's muzzle. Still no sign of the three men on the run, and he was forced to give Macauley credit for agility, despite his age. It had to have helped that he was running for his life.

"Where would they go without the cars?" Beacher asked at his elbow.

Bolan thought about it, knew there was a chance Macauley and his two companions might flee aimlessly into the woods and try to scale the fence wherever they encountered it—but then, what? They would be on foot and carrying illegal weapons, when they had to know police were on the way.

"We're missing something," Bolan said. He turned to scan

the broad lawn, saw a wink of flame downrange and felt a bullet sizzle past his ear.

They hit the deck together, seeking cover that was nowhere to be found without retreating to the house. Instead of bolting, Bolan lined up on the muzzle-flashes with his rifle's telescopic sight, held steady under fire and triggered half a dozen 5.56 mm rounds from fifty yards.

A kind of yelp reached Bolan's ears, presumably a hit. He waited several seconds more, then took a chance and rose to draw the sniper out if he was still alive.

Nothing.

"What's over there?" Beacher asked, as she scrambled to her feet.

"The loch," Bolan replied. "Macauley's chairlift and the stairs."

"But why run to the water?" she inquired. "You sank the *DeepScan* and their submarine."

An automatic weapons stuttered in reply to Beacher's question, but the shots weren't meant for them. They were well away beyond their line of sight, in fact. And as they moved in that direction, cautiously, an engine growled, its rumbling rising up to greet them from the loch below.

"I missed a boat," Bolan said, as he reached the brink and saw a speedboat leave the boathouse, veering sharply to the north. Below, an unfamiliar craft was nosed against the listing *DeepScan,* with a body sprawled across its deck.

"The water bailiff," Beacher said. "They've shot him."

Bolan started down the stairs, passing another body on the way—the sniper, their would-be murderer, another failure in the laird's service.

"Let's hope they didn't hit the engine," Bolan called back to Beacher. "We still aren't finished here."

THE SPENCER RUNABOUT was small by lairdly standards, but it boasted twin 450-horsepower Crusader engines with a top speed of sixty knots—approaching seventy miles per hour.

When he took it out, say once a month in spring and summer when he had the time to spare, Macauley enjoyed the rush of wind in his face and the snarl of the motors behind him, carving their wake on a mythical monster's domain.

On this night, with any luck at all, the little boat would save his life.

Macauley still had no idea who was responsible for the attack on his home, or any of the other recent incidents. It galled him, but if he escaped—*when* he escaped—there would be time to puzzle over it and mount his own investigation, while solicitors defused the ticking bomb of charges that police were bound to file against him.

He had explanations already in place for everything. A recognized eccentric in the grand British tradition, he would cheerfully admit his gullible participation in a treasure hunt. Of course, he didn't know the men he'd hired to run the operation were suspected terrorists who'd bring their urban war from Glasgow to his very doorstep. It was the responsibility of law enforcement to identify such men and take them out of circulation.

As for Jurgen Dengler, certainly he'd known the man had fought for Germany, some sixty years past. So had countless others, including some revered postwar statesmen. Again, if Dengler was a hunted Nazi criminal, why wasn't he arrested at his home in Switzerland? Why was he free to travel throughout Europe unimpeded? No one could reasonably ask Macauley to usurp the role of Interpol or Scotland Yard in tracking fugitives.

The treasure? Why, of course he'd planned to let the rightful owners have their due, but how could he proceed when unknown saboteurs had wrecked his exploration vessel and submersible? If someone else wanted to raise the U-boat, they were welcome to it, by all means.

But first, escape.

"Where are we going?" Gibson asked him, voice raised to be heard over the speedboat's twin engines.

"Inverness Marina," Macauley said. "I've a berth there, fifteen minutes from the airport."

"And from there?" Gibson prodded.

"I haven't decided," Macauley replied. Thinking to himself that Gibson wouldn't be going with him.

It was time to sever all unhealthy ties, for his own good. In fact, it would be helpful if the TIF commander tumbled overboard—perhaps as they were passing Urquhart Castle, where the loch was deepest.

Rest in peace—or pieces, as the case might be.

THE WATER BAILIFF'S Chris-Craft Launch was built for chasing speeders on the loch and overtaking poachers who were anxious to avoid arrest. Once Bolan had shifted the officer's body and settled in the driver's seat, he found it easy to control, with a satisfying kick from its Mercury 260-horsepower engine.

Given Macauley's speed and lead time, Bolan wasn't sure that he could overtake the runners, but he could certainly keep them in sight, close the gap and hope for a shot with the Steyr AUG.

No speedboat ever made could outrun bullets.

"I never thought about a third boat," Beacher said.

"Neither did I," Bolan admitted. "Nothing we can do about it now, but try to get in range."

"And then?"

"You take the wheel and hold it steady, while I try to slow them."

"Kill them, you mean," she said.

He didn't answer. There was no more to be said.

"And if we can't, what then?" she pressed.

"Follow and find out where they're going. Take them on the dock, wherever. One way or another," Bolan said, "it ends tonight."

They raced on through the darkness, tracking Macauley's wake by moonlight, chasing the noise of his speedboat's engines. They were still northbound and well out toward the middle of the loch, instead of following the eastern shore. Bolan took for granted that Macauley knew where he was going, that he might've called ahead to have a car and extra shooters waiting on arrival.

Drumnadrochit? Inverness? The chances of escaping would be better from the larger city, with its high-speed motorways and an international airport nearby. If a private plane or charter flight was standing by, Macauley could be out of Scotland by the time police began to look for him in earnest.

If he lived that long.

But they were getting closer, the noise from Macauley's twin engines loud in Bolan's ears. Three hundred yards and closing. Did the runners even know that he was coming up behind them, running without lights?

"Be ready for the wheel," Bolan said, as he kept the throttle open, running up Macauley's wake. "It won't be long, now."

"Ready when you are," Beacher replied above their engine's roar.

Bolan was on the verge of rising from his seat, lifting the Steyr and surrendering control of the vessel, when something happened up ahead. He registered a burst of moonlit spray, and then Macauley's speeding boat was airborne, rising almost vertically before its hull exploded, shards of fiberglass filling the air like shrapnel.

Bolan throttled back, holding enough speed to prevent his boat from stalling, as the remnants of Macauley's craft came splashing back into the loch. Its engine swamped and sank at once, while other wreckage lingered on the surface, swirling, slowly going down.

Beacher switched on the spotlight, swept the water with its brilliant beam in search of swimmers, finding none. Bolan circled the area, saw nothing to explain the leading boat's dramatic self-destruction. Had it struck a wave? A floating log that went down with the wreckage?

Something else?

"There's nothing left," Beacher said moments later.

Grim-faced, Bolan turned the launch around and headed south.

Epilogue

"What about Dengler?" Bolan asked Beacher. She'd spent most of the early morning with police milling around Macauley manor and its grounds, returning to the lodge with a weary air and looking miffed to find Bolan napping on the big four-poster.

With the Beretta 93-R close beside him, just in case.

"They found his wheelchair," she replied, while making coffee for herself. "Bloodstained, but no sign of the man himself, so far. My guess, he crossed Macauley somehow or the laird decided not to share his booty. They'll be bringing in cadaver dogs later today. He'll be around the property somewhere."

"Maybe together with the ghillie," Bolan said.

"Unless they buried him at sea," Beacher replied.

BBC Scotland had the early news on television: mayhem at Loch Ness, details and video to follow. The police were not releasing any names so far, but the news reader floated speculation of involvement by the Tartan Independence Front. Already, there were rumblings of a parliamentary investigation into homegrown terrorism and the proper methods of suppressing it.

In reality, the hard decisions were never made in public, by committee. Action sprang out of necessity—and if conducted properly, it ceased when clear and present danger was eliminated.

For the moment, anyway.

"What do they think about Macauley's accident?" Bolan inquired.

"For now, the party line is that his boat collided with a floating log, maybe a wave," Beacher replied. "It's John Cobb all over again."

"And his reason for running?" Bolan asked.

"The fight at his house," Beacher said. "They're not prepared to say he was a part of it, just yet. Perhaps a target of the TIF because he spurned demands for financing."

"That's rich."

"*He's* rich. Or was, at least. It goes against our grain to bruise aristocratic toes."

"Even when they have feet of clay?"

"Don't worry," Beacher said, sipping her coffee. "The truth will come out over time. Well, most of it. Dengler's involvement will delight the tabloids, once it leaks. Our part will be submerged by the *Official Secrets Act*."

"Just like Macauley in the loch," Bolan observed.

"They'll likely never find him," Colleen said. "Or Gibson. You know what they say about Loch Ness keeping its dead."

"The cold water," Bolan said.

"Or something."

"Right. Still time for breakfast," he remarked, "before we hit the road."

"I have some people coming up," Beacher replied. "I'll ride back to London with them."

He nodded. "So, no appetite after last night?"

"I wouldn't say that," she replied. "But they serve breakfast until nine, and checkout is at noon. I thought…"

"What?" Bolan asked.

"That maybe we should both go back to bed."

Why not? Respites from death were few and far between in Bolan's world. Why shouldn't two consenting soldiers find a little comfort in the wake of battle, with a victory in hand?

"Suits me," he said. And smiled.

* * * * *